FOUL*PLAY*

Tom Palmer is a football fan and a writer. He never did well at school. But once he got into reading about football – in newspapers, magazines and books – he decided he wanted to be a football writer more than anything. As well as the Football Detective series, he is the author of the forthcoming Boys United series, also for Puffin Books.

Tom lives in a Yorkshire town called Todmorden with his wife and daughter. The best stadium he's visited is Real Madrid's Santiago Bernabeau.

Find out more about Tom on his website tompalmer.co.uk

FOUL
PLAY

TOM **PALMER**

PUFFIN

PUFFIN BOOKS

Published by the Penguin Group
Penguin Books Ltd, 80 Strand, London WC2R ORL, England
Penguin Group (USA) Inc., 375 Hudson Street, New York, New York 10014, USA
Penguin Group (Canada), 90 Eglinton Avenue East, Suite 700, Toronto, Ontario, Canada M4P 2Y3
(a division of Pearson Penguin Canada Inc.)
Penguin Ireland, 25 St Stephen's Green, Dublin 2, Ireland (a division of Penguin Books Ltd)
Penguin Group (Australia), 250 Camberwell Road, Camberwell, Victoria 3124, Australia
(a division of Pearson Australia Group Pty Ltd)
Penguin Books India Pvt Ltd, 11 Community Centre, Panchsheel Park, New Delhi – 110 017, India
Penguin Group (NZ), 67 Apollo Drive, Rosedale, North Shore 0632, New Zealand
(a division of Pearson New Zealand Ltd)
Penguin Books (South Africa) (Pty) Ltd, 24 Sturdee Avenue, Rosebank,
Johannesburg 2196, South Africa

Penguin Books Ltd, Registered Offices: 80 Strand, London WC2R ORL, England

puffinbooks.com

First published 2008
Published in this edition 2008
1

Text copyright © Tom Palmer, 2008
All rights reserved

The moral right of the author has been asserted

Set in Sabon
Typeset by Palimpsest Book Production Limited, Grangemouth, Stirlingshire
Made and printed in England by Clays Ltd, St Ives plc

British Library Cataloguing in Publication Data
A CIP catalogue record for this book is available from the British Library

ISBN: 978-0-141-32579-8

www.greenpenguin.co.uk

For Mum – wish you were here

ACKNOWLEDGEMENTS

I need to thank a lot of people for encouraging and helping me to write this book. But first – and foremost – I want to thank my wife, Rebecca, and my daughter, Iris, who have given me the self-belief and time to do it. If Macmillan Cancer Support hadn't brought us together, this book would not exist.

Thank you also to Alison Barrow for telling me about a literary agent who supported Leeds United; David Luxton, of the Luxton Harris Literary Agency, for having faith in the book and for calling me one day to say that my fantasy publisher, Puffin, liked it; Ian Daley of Route Publishing for saying that I should write crime fiction; Sophie Hannah, Ray French and James Nash, the Leeds-based writing group who helped develop this novel; Martyn Bedford for being a great mentor; Comma and Route, independent publishers who gave me the support to develop as a writer; Arts Council England, the Society of Authors,

CIDA and the Year of the Artist, all funders who gave me impetus, self-belief and money to write; Alison Shakspeare and her daughter VJ, Jackie Rowan, Mark Hodkinson, Ralph Newbrook and Nikki Woodman for reading the book in its early stages; Jim Sells (the Bobby Moore of literacy) at National Literacy Trust and Ralph Newbrook, who, as well as reading the manuscript, involved me in their tireless and inspired work to encourage children to read though their love of football; and – as always – to Leeds Libraries, who since I turned seventeen, have intervened, directly and indirectly, several times to make me both an enthusiastic writer and a reader.

I want to thank everyone at Puffin for the diverse and enthusiastic work they do to publish and promote books. Especially Sarah Hughes, Alison Dougal and Adele Minchin. Thanks also to Anna Billson and Sara Flavell who designed the book's wonderful cover. It is a great honour to have my name and the Puffin logo on the same book cover.

Finally, to my mum for encouraging a very reluctant reader, age seventeen, to begin to love reading through football.

CONTENTS

Sunday

Monday

FRIDAY

NIGHT VISION

Danny crouched when he heard the footsteps.

Then, after counting to ten, he looked carefully over the top of the wall through fragments of broken glass set into a line of concrete. There were two men. Both dressed head to foot in black. Both wearing ski hats low over their hair, their ears, their eyebrows.

This was it.

What Danny had been waiting for, sitting out in the cold every night for the past week. He felt excited. Or afraid. He wasn't sure which.

Danny watched the men, the tip of his nose touching the cold brick of the wall to make sure his head stayed still.

Neither man spoke. They communicated with nods and quick hand gestures.

At first, Danny couldn't be absolutely sure the two men were not just drinkers returning late from a night out, nipping round the back of the shops to relieve themselves. But it would have been a coincidence that it was the back of an electrical store at three in the morning, in the same month that a dozen other similar shops had been burgled.

Anyway, whatever they were doing, they wouldn't take kindly to being watched by a fourteen-year-old boy.

Danny held his breath as the two men studied the door and windows, shining a torch through one. The beam of the torch highlighted the red brick of the buildings, a shining black drainpipe, paint-peeling window frames. It was a typical rundown back alley. Boarded up windows on the building next door. Roof slates caught in the guttering above. Broken glass underfoot, which Danny could hear crunching as the men trod on it, probably from discarded bottles that were strewn about the back of the terrace of shops.

Behind Danny there were a hundred metres of open ground: dog-walking grass and makeshift playing fields. And, beyond that, a road with a vehicle coming every thirty seconds or so.

Suddenly one of the men looked straight at Danny.

Danny didn't move. Not at first. He kept his head absolutely still. He didn't dare breathe. Carefully, he shifted his feet into a position he could launch himself from.

The man looking towards him was short. Quite thin.

Small features on his face. A moustache. Eventually the man's eyes turned from Danny towards the bag at his side. He'd not seen Danny. Maybe he'd just sensed him.

Danny watched him pull a long piece of metal out of his bag − a crowbar − then begin to touch the window frame, pressing it with his gloved hands, presumably looking for a weakness. The other man − tall, powerfully built, younger-looking − was standing next to a black wheelie bin, his back to a door, scanning the passageway he'd just come down. The smaller man began to jemmy the window, hacking at the frame, forcing the crowbar blade deep into the wood, then levering it away.

This was *defnitely* it.

Danny took out his video camera. His fingers fumbled as he took the lens cap off and pulled the mini-screen out to face him. He pushed the camera up his jumper to switch it on. He had practised this manoeuvre a dozen times in his room at home. To muffle the *ping* it made.

Had they heard?

Danny looked over the wall again.

The two men were still busy. So Danny checked the camera was on night sight and put it on top of the wall, the mini-screen angled down so he could see it. He felt as if he was in a submarine, peering through a periscope. It was so dark and cold it wasn't difficult to imagine himself underwater.

On the screen, he watched the smaller man levering hard at the window, working at the wood, then stopping, sometimes for up to a minute. But every time a car or truck came by on the busy road that ran on the other side of the row of terraces, the man would start again. Hacking at the wood.

Danny realized that he was waiting until a vehicle came past to lever the crowbar, shattering the window frame when no one would hear it above the rumble of an engine or tyres rattling over potholes.

Danny filmed the men, now focusing on their faces. First the one in the doorway. Then the one with the crowbar. He was getting good detail. This would be useful. Very useful.

He was shocked to see the low-battery sign come up on the mini screen. He knew he had a second to switch the camera off before it made the sound to register a loss of power. But his hands weren't quick enough.

PING. PING. PING.

Danny felt like his heart had stopped. He raised his head very slightly above the top of the wall.

The two men looked in his direction and froze for a second. Then, frowning, the larger man began to move slowly towards Danny.

Danny shoved his camera into his jacket pocket.

Then he was running.

The first hundred metres were exposed ground.

Danny saw a children's playground to his right. A row of trees to his left. His mind was empty. His chest was burning.

Since he'd set off running, he'd heard nothing except the wind in his ears. No sound of footsteps coming after him. No shouting. So, as he was about to pass from the grass on to the main road, he stopped and looked back. Was anyone following him?

He strained his eyes and ears.

Nothing.

He could feel his heart going like a hammer drill and his lungs straining so much he felt like he was still running.

No one was coming.

He was safe.

It was OK.

Then, suddenly, like an animal coming out of the dark, he saw a figure moving fast. The larger of the two men. He was much bigger than Danny. Bigger, even, than Danny's dad.

Danny turned to run again, on to the pavement, scrambling to get some speed. The feel of the tarmac under his feet was hard and painful after the soft turf of the park. He crossed the road. Squinting under the glare of the streetlights.

He went up a passageway.

It was a passageway he knew well.

Even though he didn't live around here, Danny was more familiar with this part of the city than any other. It was just two hundred metres away from the football stadium where he came thirty or more times a year to watch City. And his hero, Sam Roberts, the club's top scorer.

Danny came with his father to every home game. This was the passage Danny always led his father down. Towards the stadium. To the main stand, where he would describe the game to his dad like a commentator. Danny's dad was blind.

But Danny knew that his dad and football were the last things he should be thinking about. He cleared his mind.

His ankles jarred as he ran. He could hear the man running now. Both their footsteps echoed off the walls of the passageway, putting Danny off his rhythm.

He was terrified, but focused on getting away from this man. Trying to ignore the thoughts of what he might do to Danny if he caught him.

There was a fork in the passageway coming up. If he turned left, he'd be in an estate: gardens and walls, lots of cover, but lots of open ground too. Right, and he'd be near the railway track by the yard with the knackered fence, full of old railway signs and abandoned Portakabins.

That was it.

He'd go in there.

Slip through one of the holes.

He was smaller than the man chasing him. Much smaller. He could get through the fence, into the yard and up on to the railway track, maybe. Then down into a factory. Make an escape.

'You'll have to run faster than that,' a breathless voice called after him. Much closer than Danny had realized.

Turning right, Danny glanced back and saw the man chasing him. He was less than ten metres away.

Danny put on a burst of speed. Saw the hole in the fence he'd remembered. A gap he'd walked past a hundred times.

Now he dived through, head first. He was doing OK ... until his coat snagged. Danny pulled harder, but he was stuck. He felt like a fish caught in a net. The footsteps following him stopped. He heard a scuffing, felt the man's hands on him, then a punch to his back.

'Where's that camera?' the man said in a breathless, soft voice, strong hands pulling at Danny.

Danny was in trouble now. But he had one more chance. He kicked both legs back, suspended, his coat still hooked to the fence. He felt the man's body give behind him, then heard him cough, winded.

Danny's coat ripped with the force of his kick and he was free.

He stumbled to his feet, both knees stinging with pain, and ran across the yard, hurdling old railway lights and coils of thick wire. He meant to go across the yard and find a way on to the railway track, but he was suddenly floodlit from several angles. Security lights. He felt exposed and decided to take a right and hide among the dozens of Portakabins.

About to enter the maze of prefabricated buildings, he looked back. He could see the man tearing at the fence, trying to get in, all the time staring at Danny. Danny held his gaze for a moment, knowing he'd have to find another way in.

They both heard the siren at the same time.

Danny supposed that he must have set off an alarm when he'd triggered the security lights.

The man had stopped tearing at the fence. But Danny could see him smiling.

Why?

Then Danny saw that the man was waving something in his hand. He tried to see what it was. A small piece of dark card? For a minute the man looked like a referee sending him off. Then Danny recognized it. The man was holding his notebook.

'I'll catch you later,' the man said, turning to jog back down the passageway as the siren of a police car wailed louder and louder.

PRIVATE DETECTIVE

Danny sat with his back to a Portakabin.

He was now right next to City Stadium, looking at the players' entrance and a fire exit from the side of the main stand. Danny had never been this close to the door the players slipped in and out of before and after the games. This was the car park – empty now – where all the Ferraris and Porsches would normally be parked.

After the chase, Danny's body was beginning to calm down. He felt exhausted. In his legs. His lungs. His head. What had he been thinking? Tracking burglars. Being chased through the streets by a criminal at three in the morning. Nearly being caught! And losing his notebook. How had that come out of his pocket?

Danny checked his coat. One of the pockets was torn right away.

That was how.

His mind raced through the information in the notebook. Was there anything the men could use to find him? There were newspaper clippings covering the burglaries. Flowcharts he'd drawn up himself to try to work out what the burglars were after and where they might strike next. The results of days of investigations.

It had begun with an article in the local paper. STRING OF BURGLARIES FOX LOCAL COPS. Several electrical stores had been cleaned out. Game consoles. Computers. Flat-screen TVs. DVDs. The lot. All within the city. All independent shops. None of the big chains.

As an avid reader of the newspaper's crime pages, Danny often followed all sorts of stories from the first reports, through the police investigation, the arrest of the suspects and their trials. He'd even started going to the trials, not satisfied with the sparse information in the paper.

But what Danny wanted most was to be a detective, to solve crimes himself.

At fourteen he couldn't join the police. So Danny set up his own detective agency. He called it Pinkerton's, after a famous detective agency in America. He rearranged his bedroom like an office. He got his hands on a swivel chair and an old desk. One of the desk's drawers had a lock. He kept his notebooks in there. He put up cork board on one of the walls so he could pin newspaper articles, photos and maps to keep the most important facts out in the open, always in his mind. His mum and dad had been OK with it. They indulged him. Even supported him. But they wouldn't let him buy a new bedroom door with a frosted glass window in it, with D. HARTE, PINKERTON'S in black lettering written on it.

Danny's favourite detectives were from the crime novels he took out of the library to read to his father.

His dad had read crime and detective stories since he was a boy, before he'd been blinded in an accident at work. Now Danny spent an hour reading to his father every night, joined by shadowy detectives, murderers and the lowlife of cities across the world. His dad's favourite writers were American: Raymond Chandler and Dashiell Hammett. Lots of guns and a high body count. Or the Belgian writer Georges Simenon. Danny enjoyed them, but also liked British thriller writers like Graham Greene and John Buchan.

Since he'd been reading these books, day after day, enjoying them more and more, Danny had become obsessed with crime. And its detection.

That was why he found himself video-recording burglars at three in the morning in the inner city.

His dad would kill him if he knew.

*

Sitting on the steps of a Portakabin – not wanting to go inside because of the scratching sounds he heard coming from within – Danny tried to gather his thoughts.

He noticed his arms were grazed, half a dozen red lines scored from his wrists to his elbows. Both arms. The skin had broken in places, but there wasn't much blood. It was only when he looked at them that they began to sting.

Danny wasn't afraid the burglars would be waiting for him. The police siren had been enough to scare them off. They'd have wanted to get clear of the area, rather than risk being caught. Even though he was pretty sure the police car had just been passing through, oblivious to the burglars and Danny. He'd not seen or heard anything of it since.

But Danny *was* worried that the men had his notebook. What would they find out about him? For a start, they'd know he was tracking the robberies. They might be concerned enough to try finding him. He tried hard to think if there was anything personal in the notebook, something that would lead them to him, but nothing came to mind.

Danny tried to imagine how he would feel if he knew someone was keeping a notebook about him. This was one of the techniques he'd read about in a book. The detective should put himself in the position of all the suspects. He'd find out as much as he could about them. Then imagine he was them, feeling all the things they might feel, knowing all the things they might know. Then he'd have a better idea of what everyone was thinking and what they might do.

Danny thought that the men would be glad to have the notebook and would also be glad to get their hands on him if they could. But they probably wouldn't go out of their way to find him just because of the notebook.

The problem was the video camera. His hand touched his other pocket. It was still there. The burglars had heard it ping when it ran out of power, so they probably knew he had footage.

Danny wished *they* had the camera and *he* had the notebook.

He looked back the way he'd come, to see if either of the men had returned. There was no sign of them. He listened, but he couldn't hear anything.

He leaned against the door of the Portakabin. Five more minutes to calm down – then he'd make a move.

Two minutes later, he was flooded with light for a second time.

He eased himself back into one of the Portakabins and squatted down to avoid being seen. He could feel damp through his trousers. There were more noises around him. Scuffling. Scratching. Scrabbling. He knew it was rats. He hated rats.

The new lights weren't coming from the Portakabin yard, so where were they coming from?

He poked his head out of the door. They were coming from the football club. The car park.

The facade of the stadium and the doorway into the players' entrance were lit up. Danny saw the club crest on the wall.

He watched closely, worried it was the headlights of the police car that had gone past earlier. He was trespassing, after all, and didn't want to be caught any more than the burglars did.

It *was* a car. But not a police car. And it couldn't be the burglars coming after him, not inside the City Stadium car park.

After watching for a few seconds, Danny came cautiously down from the Portakabin to see three men emerge from a black people-carrier in the car park. The driver and two passengers. The first passenger was a big man. Bald. White. Mean-looking. Danny had him down as a bouncer or a minder, something like that. He wished he had his notebook with him. There was so much to take in, to remember.

But what could he do?

He needed tricks. Memory tricks.

He remembered a film he'd once seen. *The Thirty-*

Nine Steps. A thriller about a man who has an amazing memory. How did *he* remember things? He'd match facts to objects. Then he could lodge them in his brain and draw them out when he needed them.

Danny looked at the scene.

Three men: three bins next to the door. That was easy.

Black people-carrier: black night.

He could just make out the registration. CP04 FRC. CP: Car Park. Number of wheels on people-carrier: 04. FRC. Football. Rugby. Cricket.

If the first man looked like a bouncer, the second looked like a banker. Danny stared at the third man, wanting to find some likeness for him that started with B, so he could remember it like a short rhyme. Bouncer. Banker. What?

Danny watched him closely. Something about him seemed familiar. He was wearing a bulky coat. And was much younger than the other two. Not greatly older than Danny. There was something about the way he moved that reminded Danny of someone.

Like other people, Danny could recognize people he knew from a distance as much from how they moved and walked, as by their faces and the colour of their hair. Say he saw a group of lads standing at the chip shop in the dinner break: even though everyone was dressed in the same school uniform, from two hundred metres he could tell if his best mate, Paul, was among them just by the way he shuffled along.

Danny was wondering who this familiar figure was, when the man turned towards him. Danny saw his face in the dipped headlights.

It was Sam Roberts. *The* Sam Roberts.

He'd been right about him being familiar.

Except Roberts had something over his eyes. A thin bandage? Or some trendy sunglasses? No, it was definitely a bandage.

The headlights went off as Sam Roberts walked in front of them.

Now Danny wished he had power in his night vision camera to film Sam Roberts. The best player at City. The best player in the league. He'd finished the season with thirty-four goals two weeks ago. He was on his way to play in the European Championships for England, where he could prove he was the best player in Europe. With Roberts in the team, England were second favourites to win the tournament.

So what was he doing here at nearly four in the morning?

Danny assumed Roberts had been injured. Something to do with his eyes, by the look of it. He remembered after his dad's accident. A bandage across half his head. Roberts's had been a thin bandage

– just covering his eyes – but it looked bad. Why was he being taken into the stadium this late? Wouldn't it make more sense to go straight to hospital?

Danny watched the three men go into the stadium. The bouncer opened the door – there seemed to be more people inside. Two at least. Danny couldn't be sure. Then Sam Roberts went in, led by the banker.

The door into the stadium closed and Danny was left alone.

What now?

There was so much to think about.

Danny was not worried about the burglars any more. They'd have come for him by now, if they'd wanted to.

But he desperately wished he had his notebook. All the things he'd recorded in it, lost. And so much more he wanted to remember. The chase. What the burglar had said. The scene that he'd just witnessed outside City Stadium.

The sky would begin to lighten soon. A grey twilight before the sun broke over the horizon and the air warmed up. Danny knew this time of day well after one or two other nights staking out electrical stores.

The night had brought him more than he imagined it would. Enough to *fill* that notebook. He would go home via the twenty-four-hour petrol station, buy a new notebook and write everything down before his mum and dad got up.

Then he had to decide what to do about what he had seen.

The burglars he had on film: should he show the police now?

And Roberts? He had to find out what was going on.

HAPPY FAMILIES

'You were up early.'

Dad smiled as he came into the kitchen.

It was medium-sized for a kitchen, with room for a small table and three white-box kitchen appliances. They'd had a new kitchen put in five years ago, but the chipboard kitchen units were already warped by water. And there were too many mugs. Mugs in cupboards. Mugs on mug hooks. Mugs on the mug tree. Danny's dad weeded the mugs, threw away the older ones without telling his mum. But this just made room for the new ones his mum bought or was given as gifts.

When he came in, Danny had been staring out of the window, watching cars on the main road. His dad was wearing a blue dressing gown tied at the waist, with brown pyjamas underneath. He was a tall man with a beard and a red complexion.

Did he know Danny had been out most of the night?

Danny had been sitting at the table for over an hour, scribbling in his new notebook, trying not to forget anything. He had used the memory tricks to recall the black people-carrier, the three men, the car's registration number. Now he was imagining he was there again, trying to capture every detail, the burglar, the Portakabins, Sam Roberts. If he could remember smells and sounds and even the cold air, it would trigger other memories. He'd heard a crime writer say that once on TV. Use your five senses.

'I had a bit of homework to do,' Danny said, realizing his dad was waiting for an answer.

Since his dad had lost his sight, Danny had always tried to be straight with him, but today he was anxious. So he lied.

He regretted it immediately.

'You should have done it last night, Danny. Then you could have relaxed. You sound tired.'

Danny didn't say anything. Dad took the teapot, weighed it in his hands and went to the sink to empty the old teabags out of it.

Danny felt guilt at his small lie. He remembered the day he came home from school. Six years ago. The door had opened as he came up the garden path. And he'd been surprised to see his granddad.

'Your dad's in hospital,' he'd said. 'He's had an accident. On the job.'

Danny remembered his granddad's words and the sound of his voice, as if it were only yesterday.

'In a fire?' Danny said. His father had been a fireman.

'I don't know,' his granddad had said. 'There was some sort of explosion. That's all your mum's been able to tell me.'

'Is he going to be OK?' Danny had said.

Granddad's reaction had stayed with him forever. He'd opened his mouth, but had been unable to speak, so he'd just shrugged. Dad could have died that night.

'Is everything OK? Danny?' Dad's voice brought him back from his memories.

'Fine, Dad. Yeah.'

Dad said nothing. He continued to chop the apple he'd already peeled and cut in half.

Danny's mum came into the kitchen. She was dressed in a smart black jacket and skirt with a light blue blouse open at the neck. Her hair was brown and shoulder length. Shiny and neat. She was about to go to work.

'Emily's still in the bathroom,' Mum said. 'I have to go in ten minutes.'

'Do you want me to call her?'

'No. It'll only wind her up. I'll give her five minutes.' Mum turned to Danny. 'You were awake early, Dan.'

'Homework,' Danny said, stuffing his notebook into his school bag, an army surplus backpack.

'Industrious lad,' Dad said.

'Good,' said Mum, distracted, tipping muesli into a bowl and saying, 'Thanks, love,' when Danny's dad dropped chopped apple over it as she poured on milk.

They all went quiet as they heard Emily coming down the stairs. Seven thumps as she took the steps two at a time.

Emily was two years older than Danny. Sixteen. Going on six. There had been times when they had got on. When they were younger. He remembered holidays, birthdays. But now it was harder. The problem was she was so unpredictable. One minute she'd be kind and lovely to him; and the next she'd be horrible. Now she was in year twelve at school she lorded it over Danny, finding ways to embarrass him. And when she had her gang of mates round, they would make him feel like he was just a kid.

'I wish you wouldn't bang on the door while I'm in the bathroom, Mum,' Emily said, pushing the kitchen door open so it ricocheted against the side of the worktop. She was an inch taller than Danny. Her hair was dark and straight. She wore a white shirt. Her eyes were black with make-up. Her nose was pierced, displaying a tiny diamond. Most of Danny's mates fancied her.

'It was getting late,' Mum said.

'It annoys me.'

'So does you making me late for work, love.'

Emily took a Frosties box and shook some into a bowl. The milk she poured hit the spoon and splashed across the table.

Danny laughed.

'What's so funny?' Emily shot at him, narrowing her eyes.

'Nothing.' Danny grinned.

'I'll tell you what's funny, Danny,' his sister said. 'You mooning around Charlotte Duncan at school. That's what's really funny.'

Danny's mum carried on eating. His dad measured tea out into three mugs. Danny looked at the table. He felt his cheeks go red and a fierce heat in his head.

'You should see him, Mum . . .'

'Stop it, Emily. You're not being fair. If you want a lift to school, you'd better come now. Are you coming, Danny?'

'I'm walking,' Danny said. 'Thanks.'

He didn't want to share a car with his sister. Nor arrive at school with her.

He looked at Emily.

She was grinning at him like she'd scored a victory.

Danny was bursting to blurt out that he had seen

her smoking two days before. Mum and Dad would go mad with her. He put two fingers to lips and mimicked smoking.

She narrowed her eyes again, but Danny could tell she was worried.

Danny nodded and raised his eyebrows so only she could see, and left the room.

CHARLOTTE DUNCAN

Danny walked across the park to get to school.

The park was huge: half wooded, half open grasslands. When he was younger, he used to cycle through it with his mates, wearing away a track with his tyres, a circuit through woods and along the river that could be done in under twenty minutes on a dry day. He walked across the fields, skirting the woods, his shoes darkening as they collected dew from the grass. He didn't care that his feet were beginning to get wet; they'd dry at school.

Danny was thinking about what his sister had said about Charlotte Duncan. Yes, he fancied her. She'd been top in his league of which girls he fancied at school since the day she joined in year eight. His fantasy was that one day he'd meet her walking across this park, maybe with a dog, and the dog would be running free, or drowning in the river. At which point he'd jump in, save it and take it back to her. Then she'd like him.

Danny walked briskly through the park, coming out at the main gates, past the tennis courts towards a row of posh houses he had to walk round before getting into the estate where his school was. One of the posh houses belonged to the City chairman, Sir Richard Gawthorpe. Danny loved walking past his house. And his slick red Mercedes.

Sir Richard had been born and bred right here and had never moved away. He was a City man. That's what he prided himself on. And Danny felt just the same. He never wanted to leave this place. He loved it. Sir Richard had started a small business, developing his father's rag-and-bone round and now it was the region's biggest scrap dealer. Skips and trucks across the city bore his name. As did the high walls of his scrapyard near City Stadium. Danny could still remember the day Sir Richard had been to his school to talk in assembly. He'd spoken about having an ambition and doing *everything* you could to realize it. He talked about giving something back to the place you came from. That was why he'd bought the football club ten years ago from a white-bearded old man who had driven it into the ground. Since Sir Richard had taken over, the club had been promoted to the Premiership, played in Europe for the first time in thirty years and had its first full internationals in the team for a generation. He'd also created the academy that had scouted and developed Sam Roberts.

Danny worshipped Sir Richard.

He looked over the high garden wall draped with ivy, up at the windows and their net curtains. He'd never seen Sir Richard in there, never seen anything move inside the house, but he hoped one day he would. Maybe he'd meet him in the street. Say good morning. The closest he'd got so far was seeing him fill his Mercedes with petrol at the garage down the road. And the visit to his school assembly.

Danny carried on, crossing the ring road, walking uphill through the estate where most of the kids from his school came from. He kept his eyes straight ahead.

The wind had dropped and he took off his blazer. It was June. Soon he wouldn't have to drag the blazer to and from school with him. Soon he wouldn't have to go to school for six weeks. He couldn't wait.

In maths, Danny felt more tired than he'd ever felt before. Last night was catching up with him. Sitting here in the light of day, it didn't seem quite real. He could have easily imagined it was just a story he'd read in one of his dad's books, if it wasn't for the scratches on his arms to remind him of the fence he'd come through.

Danny didn't like maths. It was boring. He tried to

imagine what use equations and pie charts could ever be in real life. Parallel equations. Logarithms. Trigonometry. It didn't make sense to him.

He had once suggested to the teacher that they should do football league tables, fantasy football and the Opta footballers' indexes. He understood them. But someone had groaned behind him and he'd never mentioned it again.

After maths, he walked down the corridor with Paul. The corridor was packed with people pushing against each other as they walked in opposite directions. Paul supported City too. If they weren't playing in a game, they talked about City in between lessons and over lunchtime.

Recently Danny had thought about asking Paul if he'd like to come down to the law courts with him one day, but he wasn't sure if Paul would think it was strange, so he kept it to himself.

'Did you hear the thing on Five Live this morning?' Paul said.

'What?'

'There's a press conference at City this morning. Something about Roberts.'

'Sam Roberts?' Danny said.

'No, Julia Roberts, stupid,' Paul said. 'They reckon he might be injured. That's what they said on the radio. That he might miss the European Championships.'

'What?' Danny said. His mind was back on last night and seeing Roberts going into the stadium at four in the morning. Maybe he *was* receiving treatment, then. It had to be his eyes. Danny felt like telling Paul, but he didn't. He wasn't sure he could tell anyone. Not yet. Something about it didn't feel right.

There were twenty-two days to go before the European Championship finals. With Roberts, England was one of the favourites; he'd scored fifteen of their last eighteen goals. Without Roberts, they had no chance. That's why Radio 5 was so interested. The press conference could mean only one thing: an announcement that Roberts wasn't playing. Surely? So why did they need a press conference? Maybe he was all right, but, if he was, why had he been taken into the stadium in the middle of the night?

Danny had to know.

'Do you want to go?' Danny said.

'Where?'

'The press conference. I bet we could get in.'

'It's at eleven. In an hour. Double chemistry, remember?'

'Exactly.'

Danny was half joking. He'd never knocked off school. He knew the lads who did knock off. They went drinking at each other's houses. Shoplifting. Danny wasn't into all that. But today was different.

Paul said something back to Danny. But Danny didn't hear him.

Then he felt Paul nudge him, trying to get a response.

But Danny had seen Charlotte Duncan coming the other way. And Charlotte Duncan was grinning.

Danny looked at her. She had brown hair that settled on her lower neck and shoulders. Her cheeks were slightly pink. Her eyes blue. Her skin was lightly tanned, like she'd been on a sunbed or an early summer holiday. She made the school uniform look good. She wore her tie short and loose, her top two buttons undone. Danny glanced at her, then looked away. Sometimes it was too much to look at her.

Charlotte had two friends with her: Sally Graham and a girl whose name Danny didn't know. Sally was holding out a piece of paper. To Danny.

Danny watched the three girls coming towards him and, as he took the slip of paper, he caught a mocking look in Sally Graham's eyes. Then laughter from the three girls as they passed by.

'What's that?' Paul said.

'Nothing.'

'It's a note. What does it say?'

Paul led Danny into the boys' toilets. There were two year sevens there, but they cleared off as soon as they saw Paul and Danny.

The toilet smelled of urine and disinfectant. Light streamed in through the windows three metres above the row of twelve urinals. There was also a smell of paint, where the caretaker had painted over the latest graffiti.

'Read it. Does she fancy you? Look at your hands. They're shaking like mad.'

Danny unfolded the piece of paper. It was a sheet torn out of an exercise book.

Your sister says you fancy Charlotte.
Do you think she'd want your face
anywhere near hers?
Go and boil your head!

'That's sick,' Paul said.

Danny said nothing. He crumpled the note and threw it on the floor, then changed his mind, picked it up and stuffed it in his pocket. He felt angry and confused and ashamed all at once. His stomach ached so much he thought he might have to sit down on the floor. He couldn't look at Paul. Nor speak.

He had to get away.

'Come on. We have to go to the science block,' Paul said.

'I'm not going,' Danny muttered.

'What?'

'I'm going to the press conference instead. I'm not staying here. I'm never coming back. I hate it.'

'They're just having a laugh, Danny. They'll feel bad about it now.'

'No, they won't.' Danny looked at Paul. 'Seriously. I'm going. Are you coming?'

'I can't knock off.'

'OK. Will you cover for me? Say I was sick? I had to go home?'

'Sure. If you want,' Paul said. Then adding, as an afterthought: 'And text me if you find out about Roberts.'

Danny stormed out of school. He walked with purpose. He knew that if he *looked* suspicious, people would *be* suspicious. Half of him didn't care if he got caught. He'd just keep going. Make up some lie, so they couldn't stop him. A dead grandparent. A dead pet. A dead *sister*.

Going past reception, he kept his eyes ahead. But there were half a dozen others coming in and out, so he was nothing unusual. There were eighteen hundred pupils at his school. No one would notice one boy slipping away.

Danny walked to the car park, trying to look like he was going to be collected. Then he doubled back across the school fields towards the main road to the bus stops into town. And City Stadium.

KIDNAPPED

'I have an important announcement to make.'

Sir Richard Gawthorpe was standing behind a table, flanked by a well-decorated and frowning senior policewoman and a man wearing a very expensive suit, both seated. The table was covered in a white tablecloth. Three black microphones leaned towards the speakers, their wires snaking to the floor under the edge of the tablecloth. Behind them was a background of logos: the club badge, the team sponsor and Gawthorpe Recycling's logo.

Danny couldn't believe he was here. At a City press conference. Watching Sir Richard in the flesh. He'd seen them on TV, read about them in newspapers, but never imagined he'd be there at one.

Danny arrived as Sir Richard and his two colleagues passed through the door. Fifty to sixty people had followed them in. A crush that reminded Danny of dinnertime at school. He slipped in unseen and sat at the back next to a man in an open-neck shirt and black suit, with dark, gelled hair. Danny watched the journalists, the TV crews and the technicians setting themselves up. The cameras were smaller than he'd thought they'd be. Not the massive ones you might see in TV studios. And everyone looked younger than he'd expected. All he'd ever seen were newsreaders in their fifties. But most of these journalists seemed like they were in their twenties.

Danny felt safe at the back of the room. He hoped no one would notice him.

Why should they? All eyes were glued on Sir Richard. In his sixties, but well preserved, he was wearing a dark blue pinstriped suit. His grey hair was swept back, his skin tanned. Danny noticed a thick gold bracelet slip down his wrist as he dusted his hand across his shoulders. He exuded confidence. This was his place and he knew exactly what he was doing. Danny felt thrilled to be in the same room as Sir Richard. His hero – after Sam Roberts. There was something about him.

'Yesterday,' Sir Richard went on, 'we received a call from the England manager to ask why the City player, Sam Roberts, had not joined the England team for the Denmark game.' Sir Richard glanced at the policewoman who nodded at him without losing her frown. 'We contacted his agent, who also had no idea of his whereabouts. We tried to contact Sam himself. But he was not answering his mobile telephone.'

Danny wondered where all this was going.

Yesterday?

If all this had gone on yesterday, this would surely end with Sir Richard saying they'd found Sam Roberts and brought him to the stadium at 4 a.m. and all was well. But what was going on? Was he injured? What about his eyes? What had happened to him in between going missing and being brought to the stadium in the middle of the night?

'First thing this morning . . .' Sir Richard cleared his throat, looking down at his notes and sighing. 'First thing this morning, we had a call from an organization calling itself the I.K.G.P.' Sir Richard paused to stare at the cameras and journalists. His face looked drawn and Danny saw his left eye twitching. 'They claim to have kidnapped Sam Roberts and say that they will not return him until the club – or I – pay them ten million pounds.'

Sir Richard looked again at his audience – their microphones, their cameras, their mobile phones – then stepped back. The policewoman stood to allow him into his seat, where he sat, his eyes cast down at the papers in front of him.

For a second no one said a word.

Then the noise was deafening. Fifty journalists

asking questions at once. Cameras flashing.

Who had received the call?

Had Sir Richard said he would pay?

Would this jeopardize England's chances in the European Championships?

Who were the I.K.G.P.?

Were they terrorists?

Had Roberts' family been informed?

The policewoman answered the media's questions.

Sir Richard had received the call. There was no comment on whether he would pay the ransom or not. Nobody knew who the I.K.G.P. were. Yes, Roberts' family had been informed. They were present in the stadium, but had declined the offer to come to the press conference.

Danny sat in disbelief at what he had just heard. His thoughts were all over the place. He'd wanted to put up his hand and say to Sir Richard that he didn't have to worry about a thing, that he'd seen Sam Roberts coming into the stadium at four that morning, that all they needed to do was look for him. But intuition told him to think again. He'd learned this. Private detectives watch, say nothing, then head off to think before they act.

Danny had seen press conferences on the TV. This was probably going out live on one of the Sky Channels.

It'd be on the lunchtime news, in the evening papers, on *Newsnight*; then the story would hit the next day's newspapers. And who knows, there might be more news by then.

And what news?

Danny felt shaken. He knew something that no one else seemed to know. Or did he? Sir Richard's story didn't make sense if Sam Roberts *had* been brought here. And he *had* been brought here.

Danny was sure Sir Richard wouldn't lie. But he knew what he'd seen. What if he was to go up to Sir Richard and ask for a word? Would he listen? Maybe. But if Danny told him exactly what he'd seen last night the newspapers would get hold of his name and the burglars might be able to trace him. He might get done for trespassing on the Portakabin yard. And for truancy. Except it wouldn't be him who got into real trouble. It'd be Mum and Dad. And how would *they* take the news?

That was why Danny had to think before he spoke. That and the fact that whatever was going on was way above his head and he didn't have a clue what else it would bring to his door.

His dad would have loved this. He'd have said something like, 'Are you so sure about Sir Richard now?' If he'd been here. And if he'd been outside the stadium like last night. But he hadn't. And Danny was sure Sir

Richard was straight up. He'd brought the club so much success. He would have sold the stadium to developers if he was so dodgy.

The press conference ended.

As the room cleared, Danny sat wondering what to do. Should he leave? Would he be spotted? The senior policewoman was still there. Half the journalists had raced off. The other half were talking in low but excited voices into their mobile phones.

Danny was about to slip out quietly, when he felt a hand on his shoulder.

He looked round, expecting the worst.

'Are you a fan?'

'Sorry?'

'Are you a City fan?'

It was the journalist he'd been sitting next to at the back.

'Yeah.'

'Can I interview you? You're nothing to do with the club are you?'

'Yes. I mean no. I'm a fan. That's all.'

'Can I ask you a few questions? Anton Holt, *Evening Post*.'

'Sure,' Danny said automatically, still stunned by everything he had heard.

'How do you feel?'

'Me? Confused.'

'Why confused?'

Danny wondered whether to tell the journalist about the night before. But if he did he'd have to say where he'd been and what he'd been doing. He'd already decided to keep it to himself. He'd keep quiet. For now.

'I'll ask another question,' the journalist said. 'Are you worried about Roberts? What does he mean to you as a player?'

'He's everything,' Danny said. 'He's our best player. England's best player. And I don't understand why they say he's been kidnapped.' It just slipped out. Danny stopped himself from talking.

'What makes you say that?'

Danny bit his lip.

'What's your name, son?'

'Danny.'

'Danny. Is there anything you want to say to me?'

Danny was bursting to tell the journalist.

'Nothing,' Danny said. 'I'm just shocked. He's my favourite player. I just hope Sir Richard can sort it out.'

'Thanks, Danny,' the journalist said, keeping his eyes on him. 'Look. Here's my card. If you want to give me a call, feel free.'

Danny took the card and slipped it into his back pocket.

*

With the press conference room half empty and the journalist talking to an older man in a City tracksuit, Danny decided to leave. There was no one on the door. If he hung around any longer, someone might question him.

Danny walked quickly out of the room, looking at the floor, the club's crest woven into miles of thick pile carpet. He moved past glass cabinets full of small silver trophies and plaques and pendants. He'd looked at them briefly on the way in, thrilled to see them. They had names of football clubs he'd seen on Eurosport: Dynamo Zagreb, Újpest, Ferencváros. Teams City had played in the seventies, when they were briefly one of Europe's elite.

Danny went down the staircase that he thought was the one he had used half an hour before. But he soon realized he'd gone the wrong way. He was about to double back and find the proper way out when he heard voices coming from the direction he'd come.

It was two men. But not just two ordinary men. Danny immediately recognized Sir Richard's voice. The other man was clearly a journalist.

'One more question, Sir Richard?'

'Sorry, Pete. That's it. I've got to get on. Sort this out.'

'One more. Will you pay the money?'

'Pete.'

'Just this. Then I'll be out of your hair.'

'This has to be off the record, Pete. It's too sensitive.'

Danny held his breath, terrified he'd be found out. And wondering if Sir Richard would head his way after the conversation.

'I'll not be paying them a penny,' Sir Richard said. 'And that's final.'

Danny moved quietly further down the stairs, in case Sir Richard did come down. But the voices faded. The two men had gone in other directions.

Danny breathed a deep sigh of relief. He wasn't sure how to feel about overhearing Sir Richard. On the one hand he was right behind him: who were these people to blackmail City? On the other hand, shouldn't he just hand over the ten million? Danny wasn't sure. But one thing he did know was that he trusted Sir Richard – because of what he'd done for City. He was sure Sir Richard was doing the right thing based on what he knew. And what was good enough for Sir Richard was good enough for Danny.

He looked down the stairwell. The stair carpet stopped abruptly, to be replaced with concrete. Danny was faced with a double door at the bottom of the staircase.

The door was open.

Danny looked through it cautiously. All he could

see was strip lighting and a blank white corridor. Then he realized where he was.

He was under the main stand.

The very stand he'd seen the men take Sam Roberts into the night before.

DANGER – KEEP OUT

In every crime book Danny had read to his dad, the detective would, at some point, be somewhere he shouldn't. In a powerful man's office, rifling through a desk as the door handle turned. In someone's apartment in the middle of the night, creeping around so that he wouldn't be heard by a sleeping killer and his murderous cronies. Danny hated – and loved – those parts of books. His dad would always ask him to slow down, tell him he was reading too fast. But Danny couldn't help himself. Once he was reading and the story was exciting – or frightening – he needed to know what was going to happen next.

But Danny underneath City Stadium was not a story.

It was a hundred per cent genuine.

And it was also the last place Danny should be.

With senior police officers upstairs after the kidnap of one of the world's best footballers, there were probably few more sensitive places he could find himself.

But he was determined to find out more. This was too good an opportunity to miss.

There'd been a crime.

He had a lead.

And an opportunity to investigate it.

This was what he'd been waiting for for months. And it seemed more natural to him to carry on down the staircase than to turn round and head back to normality, safety and being a schoolboy.

And, if he did get caught, he could say he was lost. Play up the fact he *was* just a schoolboy.

Danny smiled.

Danny had worked out that the long corridor ahead of him ran under the bottom of the main stand, the stand he sat in at home games with his dad. This was where the players' dressing rooms were. Where they emerged from on match days, caught by the cameras before they ran on to the pitch, talking to each other, stretching, staring up the tunnel with determination. Some raucous anthem booming out in the background.

Before he began his search, the first thing Danny did was listen. He stood absolutely still and listened for every sound he could hear. He was trying to see without seeing. If he could hear anything – a conversation, footsteps, a machine – he'd know there was someone there without having to reveal his presence.

He stood motionless for five minutes, timing it to the second, breathing deeply to try to keep himself calm.

No footsteps.

No voices.

No balls bouncing.

No machines.

Nothing.

He stepped off the staircase.

The corridor was lit by a line of strip lights. The walls, ceiling and floor were painted white. As were the doors. There were no alcoves or other places anyone could hide. Now that Danny had left the staircase, if someone came out of a door they'd see him straight away. And he'd have no excuse.

But Danny thought it was a risk worth taking. He was counting on the fact that because he couldn't hear anyone, there was nobody there. He knew this wasn't certain. But it was probable. Enough to go on.

He turned left and walked carefully to the near end of the corridor, past a set of lift doors. He would search its whole length. Meticulously.

At the near end there was a large double door. It was – Danny felt sure – the door that Sam Roberts had come in through the night before. Outside would be the car park, then behind that the Portakabin yard where Danny had hidden from the burglars.

He pushed gently at the doors. They didn't move – a fire exit. He wouldn't open it; it might be alarmed. But he noted *how* to open it. A push to the metal plate. Easy. If he needed a quick exit, he'd use the fire exit rather than the stairs.

Danny turned to face the length of the corridor. Still no footsteps. Still no voices.

He started to walk.

He was even more confident that he was alone now. There was a reason there was nobody down here. The football season had finished. No players would be around. Not voluntarily. If they weren't training for the European Championship, they'd all be on expensive holidays: in the Caribbean or Australia, wherever that sort of person went. No referees either. There was no one to referee. That's why Danny could hear nothing.

Except his own footsteps.

Danny looked down at his feet and realized he was wearing his school shoes, not his trainers. Whenever he went on an investigation, he wore his trainers. They were quieter. His school shoes were making the floor squeak.

He stopped immediately, knelt down and took off his shoes. Then he loosened his belt and stuffed the shoes half way into his trousers, before fixing them there with his belt. He'd learned this in an American crime novel.

The first doors Danny came to on the corridor were labelled HOME TEAM and AWAY TEAM. He looked inside. Two square rooms. Benches going all the way round the walls. Hooks above the benches. Just what he'd expected. He tried to imagine the room full of his heroes. And the manager, shouting.

Round the corner in each dressing room there was a row of six showers. All polished chrome, they looked new, unused.

The only difference between the two rooms was that the away dressing rooms were noticeably smaller. Less room to move about. And the paint was a dull grey, as opposed to the vibrant orange of the home dressing rooms.

Danny laughed.

The next rooms were labelled KIT ROOM and INTERVIEW ROOM. Sam opened the door to the kit room slowly. He looked in. It was empty, apart from two washing machines and a tumble dryer.

The interview room was empty too. In fact, it had been stripped and the carpet pulled up, glued underlay marking the floor in ridges. The walls criss-crossed with grooves carved out of the plaster. In preparation for rewiring, Danny thought.

He let the door of the interview room close behind him.

He'd had a feeling there'd be nothing in any of the rooms.

Danny liked to trust his instincts. If he sensed a room was empty, he'd have a look. If he had a feeling there were people in it, he'd take more care. That was how he was going to do this. He trusted himself.

There were two more doors at the far end of the corridor.

The referee's dressing room – with MATCH OFFICIALS on the door – and the electrical room. Danny knew it was the electrical room because of the yellow triangle with a skull and crossbones on the door. And the sign that said: DANGER – KEEP OUT.

Like the other rooms, the referee's room was empty. Danny had known it would be. But turning to enter the electrical room, he felt differently. Something about this room made him uneasy.

THE BULLET

Danny tried the handle. But very carefully.

It didn't move.

The door was either stiff or locked. Danny didn't want to force it and risk making a sound that might draw attention. There would probably be nothing in there anyway. It was just an electrical room.

He decided to go back up the other end of the corridor to see if he'd missed anything.

Turning, he saw a scuff mark.

The floor of the corridor had been vigorously polished. That's why his shoes had been squeaking so loudly. They must have cleaned it at the end of the season after nine months of studs, mud and grass. But among all this pristine whiteness there was one scuff mark. Black. Out of place. Ten centimetres long. Right outside the electrical-room door.

An unconscious fear got the better of him. The scuff mark was something he'd not fully registered, but he knew that he couldn't leave without investigating what had caused it. It could be an important lead.

Before he tried to get into the room, he had to think. If he asked as many questions as he could and came up with an answer, however stupid they seemed, he would be better prepared.

What was the scuff mark?

A shoe? Probably. Or some piece of training equipment?

Why had it been made?

By someone running? If it was a shoe? Or someone escaping? Or something – or someone – being dragged somewhere they didn't want to go.

Had they brought Roberts here?

Danny tried the handle again.

It was still stiff, but it moved this time.

He pushed down harder, still conscious it might make a noise and betray him. But the handle gave silently.

In the electrical room there were dozens of switches with labels. A massive version of the electrical board they had at home in the cellar. The rest of the room was all wires and switches. The walls unpainted plaster.

And there was a metallic smell.

Danny knew that this was where the floodlights would be operated from. Plus the heating, air-conditioning and lights throughout the stadium.

He scanned the room again. There was nothing else. Nothing unusual. If they'd brought Sam Roberts in here, he wasn't here any more, scuff mark or no scuff mark. It had been a waste of time coming in.

Danny grabbed at the door handle, frustrated.

It wouldn't move.

'Come on,' he said, under his breath.

He tried the door again.

It was stuck.

Danny was trapped. He felt cold all over. And stupid. He could feel sweat on his hands where he'd gripped the door.

What now?

Was he going to be stuck down here until August? As the nation watched the European Championships, he'd be starving to death.

Danny panicked.

He looked around the room: four walls; no other doors; a ceiling of cables and pipes disappearing through holes upwards; a huge electrical console, buzzing.

And a trapdoor in the far corner.

He'd not noticed it the first time he'd looked.

The trapdoor was about one metre square, made of four wide planks of wood. The handle was a length of iron, dead centre. It reminded Danny of the cellar doors you could walk over outside old pubs, the place they roll the barrels down. But smaller. His hand reached out to lift it. The handle felt rough, rusty. It made a loud creak as he pulled it away.

'Boss?' A voice from nowhere.

Danny could barely breathe. He dropped the trapdoor and it bumped back into its original position.

'Boss? Is that you?'

Danny's body went rigid. Instead of running, he waited. Almost as if he wanted to hear the voice again.

It was a male voice. Deep. Gruff. Was it coming from outside the room? Or from under the trapdoor? Danny couldn't work it out.

He knelt next to the trapdoor. What would one of the heroes of Dad's books do now? He didn't know. Until he heard the sound of footsteps on metal. Maybe a ladder. Until he saw the trapdoor begin to vibrate as the footsteps came nearer.

Danny lunged for the door. He had to get out. Now. Full of adrenalin, he slammed both hands down on the stiff door handle. Mercifully, it gave and Danny ripped the door open.

'Boss?' The voice again, breathless. Then, after a pause, 'There's someone up there. You stay put. Right?'

Danny was halfway up the corridor when he heard the door of the electrical room slam behind him. Was someone after him? What should he do? Hide in another room? Go up the stairs he came from? Try the fire exit at the end?

Danny heard another sound above the noise of his panting. A click. Then a voice, a shout.

He didn't look round. He just kept running as fast as he could, his shoes still stuffed down his trousers, rubbing into his back.

All he could think about was putting one foot in front of the other. It was his best bet. He'd run at the fire escape. Push it open.

It was a risk. It might set off an alarm. But he didn't want to get caught, to have to explain why he was in this part of the stadium.

He heard the bang a split second after the wall to the left of him exploded, a shower of breeze block scattering across the polished floor. A deafening noise ricocheted the length of the corridor and back. In the moment before the bang, Danny wondered why the wall was disintegrating, why a breeze block would just explode? But once he heard the bang, he knew.

He jumped, shoulder-first, at the fire escape, his knee hitting the metal plate he needed to push to open the doors. They gave way easily.

He was outside. The cooler, fresher air hit him, filled him with hope. The light was bright, hurting his eyes, even though it was overcast. And he could hear noises. Cars on the road. Voices. Birdsong.

But above everything was the shock. And the feeling that his body was moving faster than it ever had. Faster even than when chased in the dark a few hours ago. Fight or flight. They'd done it in biology. This was flight. But not just flight. Fear too. He could feel it in his body. His heart. His lungs. His head. A tremor deep down that was shuddering through him.

As Danny ran, his friend Paul came into his mind. He'd be sitting in double chemistry now. Bored perhaps, but safe. There'd be a spare stool next to him. Danny's. Danny imagined himself there, wished he could be just a schoolboy again. Not here. Not this.

Danny moved left, to be out of sight of the exit doors. He ran through the players' car park – his feet in agony – past two TV cameras and a row of microphones all pointed at Sir Richard as he stood in front of the club crest. Another interview.

And Danny thought – though he couldn't be sure – that Sir Richard caught his eye. And for a second, in his panic, Danny felt like telling him everything. But he couldn't stop running now. He had to get as far away from the corridor as possible.

In seconds, Danny was outside the car park. Outside the stadium. On the main road, opposite the chip shop. With the corner of a building for cover, he stopped to look back, judging that no one could follow him − or shoot at him, come to that − if Sir Richard and half the world's media were looking on.

He looked.

No one was coming after him.

No one had emerged from the corridor.

Sir Richard was still doing his interviews.

And Danny wondered if the last sixty seconds had really taken place.

Danny tried to hold his body still. He exhaled and realized, leaning his back against the wall, that he'd barely breathed since the bullet had hit the wall beside him. And it *had* happened. He was sure.

Now his breathing was fast. Too fast. He felt far more uncomfortable than he should after such a short run. He was fit. He wondered if it was the shock. Was he about to have a heart attack? He'd seen it on TV. Men breathing hard, grabbing their chests, then plunging to the floor. But he knew it was just panic. What was he thinking? He had to get away from here as fast as he could.

A bus was heading down the long approach to the stadium. Danny fumbled in his pockets, trembling so much he had to struggle to find any money.

The bus arrived. Danny paid his £1 bus fare, walked upstairs and sat down.

Had that really just happened? Sitting on the bus

about to go away from City Stadium like he had a hundred times before, he wasn't so sure.

The bus moved off. Danny kept his head down, not sure if he was being followed. Why hadn't he just run over to Sir Richard and told him everything? Wouldn't that have been the easiest thing? Danny thought about it. Was it a gut feeling? Or was it proof? Yes, that was it. He couldn't just run over to Sir Richard and tell him some story without any proof. In fact, Danny thought, he didn't even know what the story was. He needed to know more. Fear or no fear, that had to be his next move.

SATURDAY

CREW CUT

The taxi dropped them off in town just before eleven. Danny stood on the kerb and waited for his dad to pay, then held his arm out to lead him into the arcade.

Today was going to be a normal day, with no burglars, no breathless chases and no bullets. Just a normal day with his dad. Otherwise Danny would go out of his mind.

It was hot already, the sky a hazy blue. Danny noticed men in shorts, women in dresses, parasols on babies' buggies. On the news the night before, the weatherman had said that today would be a scorcher.

'I need a haircut,' Danny had said to his dad after his mum had gone out.

He'd been itching to get out of the house. The shock of what had happened to him the day before was impossible to make sense of. He almost didn't believe it had happened. The more time he had to dwell on it at home the more real it might become. Someone had actually tried to shoot him. He could be dead right now if the man had been a better shot.

'Me too,' Dad said. 'Let's go into town.'

They walked through the shopping centre – past HMV, TopShop, Woolworths and Primark – to the far side of town, towards the barber Dad always used: Franco's.

There were hundreds of shoppers, walking in pairs or groups, some sitting outside cafés, chairs and tables set out in the street. Since it had been pedestrianized, the town centre had a much nicer feel to it. A gentle wind was moving up the main street. HMV was blaring out The Killers, a group of year elevens from his school stood outside listening. Danny watched the girls among them out of the corner of his eye, looking away as he came closer.

'Any more news on Roberts?' Dad said.

'How do you mean?'

'Have you heard anything this morning?'

'No,' Danny said, guarded.

'Aren't you bothered?'

'Course I am,' Danny said.

But Danny felt uneasy. He normally told his dad everything. But could he tell him he thought Sam

Roberts hadn't been kidnapped? Or that he'd bunked off school yesterday? That he'd been shot at? No chance.

'How do you feel about it?' Dad said.

'I don't know.'

'What?'

'I don't know how I feel.'

'I thought you'd be as mad as hell.'

'I'm not sure,' Danny said. 'That's all. It's weird.' He tried to think of the things his dad would expect him to say, so he could get out of the conversation without him being suspicious. 'I don't think the club has the money.'

'Sir Richard does. He's been a miser all his life. He's loaded.'

'But not ten million. I mean, that's a lot.'

'Not for him. I reckon he's got a lot more than that squirrelled away. The stuff he gets up to.'

'Why do you have it in for him?' Danny said. 'Look what he's done for the club. I don't understand why you don't trust him. He's doing everything he can. If he had the money he'd have paid up already.'

Dad said nothing. Danny noticed his half-smile disappear.

'You worship that man, don't you, Danny?'

'No. I just like him. Look what he's done for City.'

'Hmm.'

'He didn't sound like he could afford to pay up yesterday.'

'He didn't rule it out as far as I heard. Was it on the news?'

Danny cursed himself. He'd slipped up. Again. He'd heard Sir Richard talking *after* the press conference. From the stairwell. Not his official line during the interviews.

'I read it,' Danny said.

'Right,' Dad said.

Danny felt ashamed. This was the second time he'd lied to his dad in two days. Using his dad's blindness to get himself out of a hole. Here he was leading his dad through town. He trusted Danny to negotiate crossings, to get him through shops, past obstacles. And Danny never let him down with that.

It made Danny wish more keenly that he could tell him the full story. He was closer to him than anyone. But if he knew what had been going on, he'd be so worried life would be impossible. Danny would be grounded. His dad would go straight to the police. And – even though he was terrified of being shot at – Danny was excited about what was going on. And angry. He felt, at last, like a real detective. That he had come across a terrible thing, an unsolved crime. This was what he'd always wanted. All he needed was to look different and he could go back to the football stadium. This time to keep watch. All night, and the next night, if that's what it took. He'd tell his dad when it was all over. It was best for his dad. Best for Sam Roberts. And best for Danny.

But Danny wasn't convinced, despite his attempts to persuade himself.

They reached the barber's, crossing the road at the lights. It was on the ground floor of a row of tall and ornate buildings near the station that Dad said used to be the railway hotel. A place famous people had stayed, even the Queen once. But now it was a downmarket row of sandwich shops, amusement arcades and pound shops, dwarfed by the huge glass and steel buildings of the twenty-first century city.

'Peter! Peter! *Cómo está, compañero?*'

The barber was a short man with long brown hair – dyed, Danny suspected – swept back and held in place by a pair of raised sunglasses. His face was angular, a big hooked nose and a large forehead.

'Franco.' Danny's dad put out his hand.

'The usual, Peter?'

'*Sí.*'

'And Danny?'

'A crew cut, please,' Danny said.

'A crew cut?' Franco said. 'That OK, Peter?'

Danny's dad paused.

Danny watched his dad's eyes flickering under their closed lids. 'He's his own man now, Franco. He can have it cut how he likes.'

Danny felt extremely self-conscious leaving the barber's. He had always had longish hair, dark and wavy. No style to speak of. He'd never bothered with a style. And he wasn't bothered now. All he wanted was to look different to the way he'd looked at City Stadium yesterday.

He'd changed his clothes so they were nothing like the school uniform he'd worn the day before. Today he was in worn jeans and a white T-shirt. The haircut completed the new look.

'Come on. Let's go for a coffee.'

Danny said OK to his dad. He could feel the hot sun on his head as they walked. And the air. It felt good to have a short haircut on a day like this.

But he felt wary. He knew his dad could pick up on changes, inconsistencies, better than anyone — he already felt sure Dad knew that something going on. He also knew his dad wouldn't just say, 'Right, what's up with you?' But that he'd wheedle it out of him subtly, with questions and affection. This coffee could be a move by his dad to find out what was wrong with him.

This sort of thing was one of the reasons Danny loved him.

'Starbucks?'

'Starbucks.'

Dad found a seat while Danny went to get two cappuccinos and two chocolate muffins.

Once served, Danny carried the tray carefully through the maze of tables. He carried it *so* carefully, it was only when he reached the table that he noticed who was sitting adjacent to his dad, just getting up.

Charlotte Duncan.

She looked gorgeous. Shiny brown hair touching the nape of her neck. A necklace dangling at her throat.

Charlotte stood up and smiled at Danny. But not the sarcastic smile of yesterday. Something was different. Her friend – Sally Graham, there again – scowled at Danny all the same.

'What happened to you yesterday?' Charlotte said. 'I didn't see you in chemistry.'

Danny glanced at his dad and put his finger to his lips.

Charlotte mouthed, 'Sorry.'

Danny's eyes lingered on her mouth for a second too long, until he saw it crease into a smile again.

'See you on Monday?' she said, looking at his dad again, picking up several clothes-shop bags, marked H&M, Zara and TopShop.

'Yeah. See you then,' Danny said, surprised and confused.

He was thinking about the note from the day before. Maybe Charlotte hadn't known what was on it?

Danny sat down next to his dad. He could feel his heart pumping. It was going hard and fast. After a moment he noticed that his hands were still gripping the two sides of the tray.

'Now I know why you're so jumpy.'

'What do you mean?' Danny said.

'Those girls.'

'What?'

'They were talking about you.'

'Yeah?'

'While you were at the counter. I'm not sure about the other one, but the one with the deeper voice, the nice one, sounded quite pleased to see you. I think the haircut might have swung it for you.'

Danny ran his hand across the top of his head. It felt good. *He* felt good. And he was confident it was disguise enough for him to go back to City Stadium. The man with the gun hadn't seen his face. Just his clothes and his hair, from behind. Today all that was different. So long as he stayed where there were other people, he'd be fine.

And, for the first time since he'd known her, Danny felt he had a chance with Charlotte Duncan.

SCHOOLBOY

The stadium car park was jammed with huge television and radio outside-broadcast units, aerials and satellite dishes filling the skyline. Danny recognized several sports channel logos on the sides of the vans: BBC, ITV, Sky Sports, Eurosport. And there were channels from Germany, France, Italy and Spain.

It was a strange scene. Here in a shallow valley, a noisy motorway running past warehouses and out of town shopping parks, hills and fields all around them, something dramatic was unfolding.

The forecourt in front of the main stand was cordoned off, dozens of men and women were standing at its edge, some with microphones, some with notebooks. If anybody in a suit or tracksuit came out of the stadium, a series of camera flashes were followed by questions.

What was the latest on Roberts?

Was the club going to pay the ransom?

Had the kidnappers been in touch?

Outside the stadium several police cars were parked along the edge of the south stand, cordoned off by cones and guarded by a pair of police officers on horseback.

And then there were the fans. Some queuing at the club shop to buy the Roberts number nine shirts, Roberts posters, Roberts T-shirts on display in the three club-shop windows. Some hanging around, waiting to hear news of their hero. A boy in a City top, carrying a City bag. A short man with thick arms, CITY TILL I DIE tattooed on his left forearm. Two teenage girls wearing matching Sam Roberts T-shirts. Danny was among them. Keeping a low profile. Being another fan.

The chaos reminded Danny of a Champions League tie he'd been to. City against Barcelona. All the TV channels in the world seemed to be there. Plus all the newspapers. But today it was different. The fans were either queuing at the club shop or were clustered around a heap of flowers that had been piled against one of the gates to the stadium car park.

It was like a shrine, Danny thought.

Standing between the main gates, taking it all in, Danny didn't immediately hear the beep of a catering van that wanted to come past him into the car park.

Ripley Vegetarian Catering. The driver waved a thank you to Danny as he moved out of the way.

Danny waved back and smiled.

Today, he felt like a different person to the schoolboy he'd been the day before. He felt older. Things had changed.

After he'd taken his dad home, for instance, he'd gone into his local newsagent to get a paper for updates on the kidnap situation. He'd been going to this newsagent for years, but the woman behind the desk hadn't even recognized him. Then at the bus stop outside the newsagent, he'd seen two girls from his year. For a few seconds they looked at him. Then they started whispering to each other and giggling. It was only as the bus moved alongside them that one of them – looking again – gasped, 'Danny! It's you!'

The haircut had worked.

But, whether he looked older or not, he still felt nervous standing a few metres from where he'd been shot at.

He was taking a big risk.

But, last night, reading to his dad, he'd realized that to be a detective you had to challenge yourself. You had to go back to the scene of the crime again and again. You had to be there so you could see what was going on. And what wasn't going on. You had to talk to people to find out more.

That's what he was doing at City Stadium.

And – surrounded by hundreds of football fans, a dozen media outlets, cameras, microphones, journalists, policemen on horses, in cars and on foot – he was safe. And, with his new haircut and clothes, extra safe.

Now he could concentrate on doing what he had to do.

But what was a private detective supposed to do in a situation like this?

He could just watch. See what was going on. That way he'd learn a bit. But what? He wasn't sure.

On the other hand, he could make things happen.

A seasoned detective wouldn't have time to hang around, eat bags of crisps and drink a bottle of Coke. He'd be watching police movements, finding invaluable clues. He'd be talking to security men, taxi drivers, journalists.

Danny noticed the house adjacent to the gates of the football club. An old lady was standing in the garden. She looked friendly enough, watering her roses and gazing across the road at the chaos.

Danny waited for a break in the traffic, then walked across the road.

He stirred himself. This was the beginning of something big. He had to do it convincingly.

The woman had grey hair swept back into a ponytail.

She looked about sixty-five. But Danny could never tell with old people. Her garden was filled with colour. Reds and blues. Purples and yellows. The lawn was immaculate. Danny looked at her house as he approached her. He noticed that some of the wood was rotting in the window frames. That the base of garage door was overgrown with clumps of grass.

Then he walked straight past her.

He had intended to say hello, then ask her a question. But, as soon as he got near, he realized he had nothing to say. Nothing plausible. 'Hi, I'm Danny. I got shot at in the stadium yesterday and wondered if they've taken a shot at you?' just wouldn't work.

'It's all going on, love. Eh?' The woman started the conversation.

'I know,' Danny said, turning round.

The woman paused. 'Are you a fan?'

'Yes,' Danny said.

'You must be worried?'

'Yes,' Danny said.

His mind drifted again to the books he'd read. By now the detectives would have all gathered key clues from this witness. They wouldn't be answering her in monosyllables.

'Do you believe it?' the woman said.

'What?'

'Do you believe he's been kidnapped?'

'Yes,' Danny said, not sure what else he could say. The woman had put into words something that was in his mind, but that had barely come to the surface.

'Hmm,' the woman said. 'I wouldn't be so sure. You can't trust that Gawthorpe as far as you can throw him.'

'Sir Richard? Why not?' Here was someone else doubting Sir Richard.

'He's a crook.'

'Is he?' Danny couldn't believe it.

'Sure he is.' She pointed over Danny's shoulder. 'You remember those houses over there?'

'Where the Premier Car Park is?'

'The Premier Car Park!' The woman snorted. 'They make it sound so grand, don't they? Well, the Premier Car Park used to be a nice little set of terraced houses until Gawthorpe came along.'

Danny's mind fired. Now he was ready to ask questions.

'What happened?' he said.

The woman put down her watering can and took off her gardening gloves.

'There were eighteen families in that terrace,' she said. 'Fifteen of them accepted Gawthorpe's inflated money for the houses. A hundred thousand each. For houses worth eighty. Three of the families wanted to stay. So Gawthorpe arranged for one or two of the more – how can I put it – "physical" families to intimidate them. Dustbin fires at night. Cars mysteriously damaged. Poisoned pets. Two families gave in. But not Fred Hope. Oh no. He wasn't having it. He'd been through a war. He'd been on the frontline against Hitler. Some jumped up Sir So-and-so who'd only seen action at the cinema wasn't going to get him out of his house. So he stood his ground and refused to sell. Until he went to his daughter's for a week's holiday. Then his house *mysteriously* burned down.'

'Was he your friend?' Danny said gently.

'He was. He couldn't take that. Fred. His house lost like that. He said it wasn't an accident, but nobody would listen. He died soon after. Heartbroken, he was.'

The woman picked up her gardening gloves again. Her eyes were red. 'I should get on,' she said. 'Holding you up with all these old stories.'

'I'm sorry about your friend. If there's anything I can do . . .' Danny had heard people say this to the bereaved. It sounded crass. But he meant it.

'Thank you, son,' the woman said. 'You can bring me Gawthorpe's head on a plate. That'd do me.'

Danny shrugged. He didn't know what to think. Or say. He noticed tears forming in the woman's eyes. Behind her smile.

'I'm sorry about your friend,' he said again.

THE CLUE

It was time to eat. And to think.

Danny had eaten fish and chips with his dad at Hand of Cod hundreds of times. It was part of the match build-up. The bus into town. The bus from town to the stadium. Match day programme. Fish and chips. Then the match itself.

It was odd walking into the chippy. The smell of the oil and the vinegar meant match day to him and he could feel his shoulders tensing in anticipation.

'All right, son?' The man behind the counter looked at him strangely. 'Nice haircut.'

'Cheers.' Danny smiled, happy at first to be recognized – then uneasy. Would the man with the gun recognize him if the man in the chippy did? Danny tried to reassure himself, reminding himself that the gunman had only seen the back of his head as he ran out of the stand.

The chip shop had City wallpaper throughout: a

long counter of steel and glass cut the space in two, a fixture list from last season on the wall and signed photos of all the great players going back decades. Including Roberts.

The man behind the counter was very tall with broad shoulders. Although he was old – maybe even in his seventies – he was athletic looking. He had a slight foreign accent. Danny had always imagined him to be a former Eastern European footballer who had once played under the floodlights at City Stadium, perhaps during the 1966 World Cup, and had decided to settle here.

'Haddock and chips, please,' Danny said.

'Coming up.'

Danny was determined to ask some questions this time. And he knew the guy behind the counter. Sort of. He had a good excuse to make conversation.

'Have you had lots of extra customers?' Danny said. 'With all this going on?'

'We have,' the man said. 'Hundreds. We've had to step up orders to our suppliers to near match-day levels. Even in this heat,' the man said, shovelling chips into a metal scoop, then dropping them into a carton. 'I mean, I'd rather have Roberts safe and sound, but we've had more media types in here this week than in a whole year. And coppers. They like their chips, that lot. I just hope they find him, though.'

The man behind the counter took a pair of tongs and lifted a piece of battered fish on to some paper next to the chips.

Danny could smell the oil and the chips and the fish.

'Do you want anything on them?'

'No thanks,' Danny said.

Danny was just about to take the food when the man behind the counter started gesticulating.

'There it is again!' he shouted. 'Ripley Vegetarian Catering. What the heck is Gawthorpe doing getting posh caterers in for? He's always been happy enough with a haddock until now. Ten years he's been coming over here. Haddock. Chips. Red sauce. That's it. But now all the media is here, he's got fancy posh food shipped in three times a day. I'd do him a vegetable pie if he wants to be all ethical. Drives me nuts.' The man glanced at Danny and smiled shyly. 'Sorry, lad. You didn't need to hear that. Catering gets a bit competitive.'

'What? That van comes three times a day?' Danny said, wanting to tease out any detail that sounded different, even if it seemed inconsequential.

'Yep. Eight in the morning. One thirty in the afternoon. Six in the evening. Like clockwork. Breakfast. Lunch. Dinner. Stops at the gate to get a security pass. Then goes behind the entrance and along the side of the main stand. Drives me nuts. It's not in there long. Five minutes. Then it's out. Funny thing is the driver comes *here* yesterday for his dinner. Nice guy. Just the driver. Meat pie. Chips. Can of Coke. I didn't say anything. Meat pie!'

Danny sat on the wall outside the stadium eating his fish and chips. He made sure he was in the shadow of a tree. The sun was bright. Ferocious. He figured the shadow would obscure him more and he'd be able to watch without worrying about standing out.

He felt satisfied with his afternoon's work. He'd found out about Sir Richard's dealings with the locals. True or not, there was something disturbing in the woman's story about the Premier Car Park. The things he'd heard – added to what his dad always said – challenged how he felt about Sir Richard. Was he really so bad? The man that had done so much for City? Danny knew there was opinion against him. But in his heart he couldn't believe Sir Richard could be so bad. Why would he have put so much money into the club otherwise?

Why had he always thought so highly of Sir Richard? Because of what he'd done for City. And because of what he'd heard Sir Richard say about himself. About always living in the city. About how he was a self-made man. About the club.

But should he go on what someone says about himself? Or what a stranger, a seemingly nice old woman, and his own father thought of him? Or what had happened to Sam Roberts: things going on in City Stadium that the boss knew nothing about? So he said.

If Danny took away everything he had heard Sir Richard say about himself, how did things look then?

He wouldn't make a decision about Sir Richard yet. There was something more important: the catering van.

Why was the club having posh food bought in?

Danny had known immediately.

Posh vegetarian food. Sam Roberts was a vegetarian. If he was still in the stadium, it might be for Roberts. But he couldn't be there. Surely it would make no sense to keep him at his own club? And yet, Danny had been chased out of the stadium. Shot at. Something was going on.

Danny looked again at the long queue snaking into the club shop. A big window display with Roberts shirts, posters, mugs. A run on Roberts merchandise.

Danny's mind was working overtime. He had to get into the stadium. Try to find out what was going on.

He had a theory. He could tell the press, but why would they believe him? Just like they hadn't believed the gardening lady about her friend Fred Hope. And even Danny wasn't certain. He needed to prove his theory before he could do anything about it. And no one else could do it. It was down to him.

And Danny knew just the way into the stadium.

STOWAWAY

Danny pulled the back door shut, found a lever in the dark and locked it.

He'd had three seconds to make it from the Sam Roberts shrine into the catering van while it stopped for security clearance. He judged that if he made his move as a double-decker bus swept past, no one would notice anything but the engine noise and the wind the bus left in its wake. People invariably look down when a bus comes past at speed.

The bus arrived on cue and Danny lunged up the steps of the van.

It was cold inside. Very cold. Danny grimaced at the thought that he could be locked in a freezer overnight, running out of air just as the sun came up and the police found the van.

Now all he had to do was hold his nerve.

The plan was to wait for the van to stop and unload by the main stand, just like the man at the chippy had said it would, then jump out and find a way of disabling the fire-escape lock from the outside.

Simple.

This was the 6 p.m. delivery. Dead on time.

Danny moved forward in the dark, his arms in front of him. Almost immediately he hit his shins hard against something. A box he'd not seen as he scanned the space before plunging himself into darkness? Standing still, enduring the pain, his dad came into his mind.

How did he do it? Walk through town all by himself, often on new routes just to challenge himself? How could he walk alone to the toilets at half time during matches, jostled by five hundred people, and still make it back?

With this thought – in utter darkness – Danny felt scared. He wished his dad was with him. He'd be the perfect accomplice on a mission like this.

Eventually he found the back of the van and hid behind what felt like a huge rack of silver platters.

The van moved off. Forward.

Security check successful, Danny thought.

As the van moved, he tracked its movements in his head to cope with the dark. A gentle left. A gentle right. They were alongside the main stand now. Then a sudden left. But he'd expected a right to get to the main stand doors. Then the van stopped. Danny stood up, confused. The van moved off quickly again. In reverse. Danny fell, his palms hitting a bowl of wet and slimy something, what smelled like tuna all over his hands.

The van stopped. Danny fell on his backside.

He stood up and wiped his hands down his trousers, panicking. The van had not done what he'd expected. He wasn't sure he was at the side of the stadium. He knew he was near it, but he had to be on his guard, to be ready for anything.

He ducked as light burst into the van, heard the driver pick up a crate, then put it on the tarmac outside a fire exit. Danny moved to the door of the van to see what was going on. The driver had his mobile phone out. He was making a call.

'Ripley Caterers,' the man said.

Danny listened.

'OK,' the man said, leaning down and picking up the crate of food, his back to Danny.

This was the moment. Without stopping to think, Danny jumped out of the back of the van and ran for cover.

The first things he saw were three huge rubbish bins. He knew immediately where he was. The ones from last night. Three bins: three men. In the bright sunlight, they were all he could focus on. He was aware of the huge stand stretching above him. The sun hitting windows and reflecting in his eyes. But he had to move quickly. He hid behind the bins. They stank.

'Evening, mate.'

A man came out of the fire exit. Tall, muscular, shaven headed. Wearing a tight black T-shirt and jeans. He had two bags of rubbish. He threw them towards the bins. They slumped on the floor.

'All right, Andy,' the van driver said.

Danny made a mental note. Andy. The name of the man who'd come out of the stadium. Probably the man with the gun from last night.

'Bring it in,' Andy said.

The van driver picked up the food crate and disappeared into the stand with the other man.

Danny had seconds, if he was lucky.

How could he disable the door's lock?

He stood up – careful not to make a sound – and walked to the door. Inside, the two men were talking. They were twenty metres away from Danny. Danny looked at the fire exit. He'd read about doors being disabled before. Smashing a bolt. Weakening the wood. He could do neither with this door. It was a big clumsy mechanism. But there was one weakness. The hole where the bolt rested. Perhaps he could block it. But how? He looked around on the ground, desperate to find something before the guy called Andy turned round.

There was nothing on the ground. Danny grabbed at the insides of his pockets. All he had was some money, his phone and the card from the journalist he'd met the day before. He looked at it. It would have to do. Quickly, he folded the business card three times, so it was impossible to fold it any more. It was like a little cube of card. Then he shoved it into the hole and pushed it hard.

It didn't fall out.

He ran for cover.

Four hours later Danny was still outside the fire exit, his back against the wall. Everything was cooler now the sun was down. The air. The bricks. The tarmac. But the bins still stank.

Danny looked over at the Portakabin yard on the other side of the car park. He smiled. That had been two nights ago, but it seemed like half a lifetime ago. He'd been scared hiding in that yard. And he was scared now. But excited too. He wondered where the burglars were. If they'd read his notebook? If they'd acted on it? But he had other things to think about for now.

Danny checked his watch. His parents would be starting to get worried about him soon. It was way past the time he said he'd be home. And nearly ten o'clock – his deadline for being home.

He imagined he could smell fish and chips from the

chippy, just two hundred metres and a locked gate away. He was hungry again. Why hadn't he grabbed a few sandwiches from the catering van when he had the chance?

His thoughts drifted back to his parents. Should he phone them? Wouldn't it only make things worse? What could he say?

No. He'd leave it. For now.

For the first time that night the security lights in the Portakabin yard came on. Danny squinted to look if he could see anyone. What looked like a small cat moved across the yard. But he could tell by its almost skipping gait that it wasn't a cat. It was a rat. A big one. One of the rats he'd heard scrabbling around the old Portakabins while he hid from the burglars. Danny shivered, feeling even more vulnerable.

His mind kept going back to Sir Richard. His father's coolness towards the chairman. What the old woman had said. The vegetarian food coming into the ground: how could it be going on without Sir Richard knowing? The caterers. The gunman. Sam Roberts arriving in the middle of the night. It all pointed to one thing. This man that Danny had worshipped could very easily be involved. But why kidnap one of his own players? Even if Sir Richard was involved, it still didn't make sense.

Danny wanted to talk to his dad.

He took his mobile phone out of his pocket. He flipped it open without thinking. He would call home after all.

The phone rang once before it was picked up.

'Hello?' said an anxious voice.

On hearing Dad's voice, Danny realized he had to lie. Again. He didn't have a lie ready. All he'd wanted was to talk to his dad.

'It's me, Dad.'

'Where are you?'

'At Paul's. Can I . . . can I stay over?'

'You didn't say.'

'He only just asked.' Danny hoped Paul hadn't called him in the last few hours. If he had, his lie would be blown.

'OK.' Danny's dad paused before he said this. 'You'll be back in the morning?'

'Yeah.'

'OK. See you tomorrow.'

Danny put his phone away. Now he felt alone. He knew what he was doing was stupid, but it was important to him. He knew that lying to his dad was bad. This was a one off, he told himself. He sensed he was close to finding out what was going on with Sam Roberts. He imagined all the people – Roberts' family, all the City fans, all the England fans – who needed Roberts back.

Well, here was his chance to do something about it. He could sit there all night, wait for the gates to open and just walk home. Or he could do something.

He decided it was worth the lie. And that his dad – one day – would understand.

FACE TO FACE

The fire exit would not give. Danny tried to get his fingers round the edge where the two doors met. But it wasn't moving. He tried again, hurting his fingers in the gap as the door gave way a little, then snapped shut on him. The pain went right through him like electricity.

It was 11.30 p.m. The time Danny had decided he would go in.

The sky was huge and cold. With no cloud cover, the heat of the day had gone and left a thousand stars.

As Danny put his fingers round the lip of the door again he heard someone inside, coughing. He leapt away and sprinted round the back of the bins. A man emerged from the fire exit. Andy.

Danny could barely breathe, he felt so shocked.

How close was that?

The first thing Andy did was look carefully up the

side of the stadium. Then he took out a packet of cigarettes and a lighter. He sparked up.

Danny watched him breathing smoke out.

Danny had once thought that it might be a good idea if he took up smoking. Lots of detectives in his books smoked. Sitting in their offices, thinking. Standing on street corners, watching. But since his sister started smoking he realized that, as well as smelling awful, she looked stupid. Now he knew that he could never smoke. Besides, he lived his life trying not to be like his sister.

Danny watched him smoke another cigarette. He timed him. The two cigarettes took twelve minutes and forty-one seconds. Danny made a mental note. The information might come in handy later on.

Twenty minutes after Andy had gone, Danny tried the door again.

This time it opened easily. The piece of card he had stuck there had worked. Or the man hadn't shut it properly.

Danny stared down the length of the corridor. This was it. Here he was. Again.

Before he went in, he glanced at the wall where he thought the bullet had hit. There was a hole in the breeze block, exposed grey against the uniform white of the rest of the walls. He checked the floor. All the debris had gone.

He walked the length of the corridor and went

directly into the referee's room. Without thinking. Straight in.

He was banking on Andy going for another cigarette. An hour and fifty-seven minutes later – every minute of which he had counted alternatively forward or backwards, to keep himself alert – Danny was proved right.

Andy came out of the electrical room and walked up the corridor, leaving Danny with six to twelve minutes to check out the one room he'd missed in his first search.

As Andy reached the end of the corridor, Danny crept across the passageway and made his way into the electrical room. The trapdoor was up.

Now Danny felt sick. Like when you're *really* sick: weak at the knees, dizzy, dry in the throat. He had to control his breathing; it had become so erratic. What could he focus on? Meeting Sam Roberts – who he was convinced was down the ladder? Or being caught by the man with the cigarettes, Andy, who was probably also the man with the gun.

But there was no time to mess about. No time to give in to feeling sick or being nervous. He had to act. He could think later. If he got the chance.

Danny went straight to the ladder. He could feel the cold of the metal on his hands as he eased himself down. As he descended he was aware he didn't have a clue what was beneath him. A guard dog? A pack of guard dogs? Another gunman? Nothing.

He'd expected a cellar. Maybe a single lightbulb. A few shelves. Something like a handyman's room. He did not expect a large space, at least thirty metres by twenty. The place looked like a fancy loft apartment, not an underground vault. It was a large room, kitted out with expensive furniture and lighting. It was carpeted, air-conditioned. There was a kitchen bar. A gym. A circle of sofas. All open plan.

There was no one there. Just a giant flat-screen television in the corner, showing a chat show Danny didn't recognize, the sound down.

At the far end there were three doors. Bedrooms, Danny guessed. A bathroom maybe? If Danny was right, this was clearly some kind of flat. A living area. There had to be bedrooms and a bathroom.

There was a noise from above.

Danny froze, then moved tentatively to the metal steps and looked up. Nothing.

Anyway, it didn't matter. If he got caught, he got caught. He couldn't get out any other way.

That's why he had to be quick. So he *wouldn't* get caught.

Danny opened one of the doors at the end of the main space. A bathroom. As he'd thought. White fittings. Blue tiles on the walls and floor. A bath. A pile of unused towels. Two used, slung on the floor.

Danny opened the next door. A bedroom. Unlit. He tried to see if there was anyone in the bed. It didn't look like it. He flicked the light on. He had to be sure before he moved on to the next room.

'Hey!' A squinting man raised himself out of the bed.

Danny almost shouted in fear.

He knew the voice immediately.

It was Sam Roberts.

He didn't look the same as he did on the pitch, wearing the City kit. He looked normal. Except he was in a white T-shirt, his face scrunched up in the light. And he had a heavy stubble. And looked much older than he did on the pitch. Or more tired. But it was Sam Roberts all right.

Roberts' face unscrewed. He looked shocked. He wasn't wearing a bandage.

Face to face with his hero, a part of Danny wanted to go shy and quiet, but his fear of being caught overrode his feelings.

'Who are you?' Roberts said.

'I dunno,' Danny said. 'I mean. I'm a fan. I've come to get you out.'

'But you're a kid.'

Danny was terrified. Roberts was right. He was a kid. A schoolboy. He couldn't do this.

'Listen,' Danny said, 'I'm sorry to be like this, but if you want to get out of here, we need to go now. He'll be on to his second cigarette by now.'

'You know he's armed?' Sam Roberts said. 'Did you come yesterday?'

'Yes.'

'Did they shoot you? I mean, they told me they'd killed someone. That if I didn't toe the line ... You know.'

'They missed,' Danny said. 'We have to go.'

Sam Roberts got out of bed. 'OK. But where are we? Are we still in the UK?'

'You don't know?'

'No.'

Danny realized Roberts didn't have a clue he was in the stadium where he'd made his name. He must be thinking he was in some kind of mysterious bunker.

'We're right here,' Danny said.

'Where?' As he asked the question Sam Roberts' face went pale. He looked crestfallen. He was backing away from Danny, holding his hand up.

'What?' Danny said. 'Don't worry. We're leaving.'

'Yeah?' came a voice from behind Danny.

Danny turned round quickly. Andy was standing behind him, gun raised.

Danny didn't know what to do. He felt all the energy drain from him. He just stared at the man with the gun.

'You. On your knees,' Andy shouted. 'Roberts. Sit on the bed.'

Danny fell to his knees. He felt utterly powerless, only able to wait and see what would happen. He looked at the gun.

'Just sit there,' Andy said, in a quieter voice. 'Don't move.'

So Danny sat. Like a good boy. Like the man with the gun was a teacher and he'd been caught playing truant. Nothing in all the books he'd read had prepared him for this. The fear. The panic. The wave of nausea.

Andy walked backwards to the telephone. Danny watched him closely through the doorway.

The man dialled. Danny counted seven digits. No dialling code. A local number.

And Danny guessed immediately who Andy was calling.

'Boss ... Yes ... Yes, I know it's late ... I mean early ...' Andy listened, screwing up his face. 'No ... No, Roberts can't hear me ... I've ... Listen ... Roberts is here. He's OK. But there's a kid here too.' The smoker looked at Danny. 'I dunno ... thirteen ...'

'Fourteen,' Danny said. But his voice didn't sound like it normally did.

'Yes ... I'll just keep him here. You're coming? When? Now? Great.'

APPOINTMENT WITH DEATH

Thirty minutes later Danny heard the door being unlocked.

He'd been put in the home dressing rooms. A prisoner. It felt cold in the unheated underground rooms.

The first thing he'd done was check the room for possible escape routes, not bothered if he was being watched. He could see no cameras but there were no windows either. And only one heavy door, which had been locked from the outside by Andy. There was no chance of kicking it down, as it opened inwards, so he'd have to put out the whole doorframe to escape.

He really was a prisoner.

Danny sat on the benches where generations of City players had sat. It occurred to him that most fans would give anything to do what he was doing now. He smiled.

He was still sitting there when the door opened.

'Do I have to force you to come or will you just walk with me?' Andy said.

'I'll come,' Danny said.

'I won't use my gun, then.' Andy looked hard at Danny. 'OK?'

'OK,' Danny said, walking out of the dressing rooms.

Andy walked behind Danny, at his right shoulder. 'Press the lift button.'

Danny pressed it. He watched the lift floor number change on the red illuminated screen. 3 ... 2 ... 1 ... G ... B. He hadn't known there were five floors in the stadium. He wondered what they were all for. The basement was the floor they were on now. The ground floor was reception and where the press conference had been. He didn't know about the first, second and third. He assumed they were hospitality suites and offices. He was trying to put together a picture of where he was – and where he could escape to, given the chance.

The lift door opened. Danny stepped in. He half imagined seeing a trapdoor in the top of the lift, so he'd be able to jump up through it and disappear like Bruce Willis in one of the *Die Hard* films. But there was nothing.

'Press three,' Andy said.

Hospitality suites, Danny thought again. What sort of hospitality was *he* going to get?

Danny closed his eyes. He had to be calm. Hold it together. If he stayed in control, he might find a way out of this. He would pretend to cooperate. Do what they said.

Until the moment came to strike.

The only problem was, how was he going to know when the moment to strike came?

The lift doors opened at the third floor. Andy pushed Danny lightly on the shoulder. Danny started walking. There was a corridor with several heavy wooden doors. A thick blue carpet. And the smell of furniture polish and cigars.

The door at the end of the corridor was open.

Danny knew who was going to be in the room through that door. A day ago he would never have dreamed it. But, after all he had learned and seen, it was obvious.

He showed no surprise as he entered the room. He kept his face calm, although underneath he was terrified. He didn't dare guess what would happen in the next ten minutes. All he would think about was the next moment. Like the football managers say: one game at a time.

Sir Richard Gawthorpe was smaller up close than Danny had imagined. He was bent over his desk and Danny could see his thinning grey hair, a surprisingly pink scalp. He was unshaven. His clothes dishevelled. He looked tired and irritable. But then it was the middle of the night. And Danny had just got him up.

Sir Richard's desk was huge, empty of anything but a mobile phone, which was still glowing. Danny assumed he'd just finished a call.

Who to? Danny thought. Someone who needed to know that Danny had been found in the stadium.

Not the police – Danny knew that. He wished it was the police. He'd be happy to have a record for breaking and entering. He knew he was in deeper trouble than that now.

'Sit down.'

Sir Richard's voice was husky. And Danny noticed it quaver. Like his own voice would quaver when he was nervous. His hair was damp around his neck, wetting his collar, turning it a darker shade of blue.

'What's your name?'

Sir Richard asked without even looking at him.

'Danny.'

Danny had decided to be straightforward. There was no point in lying, trying to hide things. He would tell the truth as much as he could – and only lie when it was strictly necessary.

'I've seen you before.' There was no kindness in Sir Richard's voice. It was nothing like the voice he'd spoken with at assembly.

'At the press conference. Yesterday. Well, the day before. And in assembly in our school.'

Danny hoped mentioning the assembly would make Sir Richard feel sorry for him.

'Are you the one who got in here before?'

It hadn't worked.

'Yes.'

'Have you told anyone?'

Danny hesitated. This was where he had to lie.

'Yes.'

'Who?'

'I don't want to say.'

Sir Richard swivelled his leather chair round and faced what Danny realized was the pitch. With the reflections of the lights on the window from the inside, he'd not seen it, but Sir Richard was gazing across at the far side of the stadium. The stadium seemed soulless without players, fans, lights, noise.

'Because?'

'What?'

'You won't tell me who knows because . . .?'

'Because I don't know what you're going to do to me. And, if you don't know who knows, it gives me an advantage over you.' Danny couldn't believe what he was saying. Although he was nervous, he was excited to be able to talk like this to Sir Richard.

Sir Richard put his hand through his hair again. Danny watched him – and suddenly saw that the great man was confused.

Sir Richard didn't know what to do.

Danny's nerves weren't calmed by this. His heart was still going too fast and his skin felt hot. The confusion might not be a good thing. It could make Sir Richard act unpredictably.

Sir Richard was quiet for a minute. Then another minute.

'Andy,' he said finally. 'Go outside.'

Andy shook his head. 'I don't want to risk it.'

'Do it.'

'He's not just a kid. He's clever.'

'Well, give me your gun, then.'

Andy went to hand it to Sir Richard. But Sir Richard gestured towards the desk, where Andy placed it carefully.

Fingerprints, Danny thought. Sir Richard doesn't want his fingerprints on the gun. Or his DNA.

The next thought that came into Danny's head was like an electric shock: they're going to kill me.

What else would they do? The gun? Sir Richard? It was obvious.

Danny watched Sir Richard intently. He heard the door close softly behind him. He felt faint and had to grip and ungrip his hands, tighten his calves, to get the feeling back in his limbs.

'Right, Danny. Here's where it's at. You like straight talking, don't you?'

Danny didn't say anything. He felt as if he couldn't move. If he stopped holding his body so taut, he'd start to shake. Or collapse. Or worse.

'The only way I can think of getting out of this is . . . to kill you,' Sir Richard said. 'Because . . .' His voice broke into a rage. 'Because you are a stupid, meddling, nosy, over-intelligent little . . .'

Danny didn't move. Sir Richard's voice seemed remote. A long way away. And Danny could hear a ringing in his ears.

'I think I have to do that because *I* kidnapped Sam Roberts and because *you* know. And, if I don't kill you, then the secret is out.'

Neither said anything. Danny noticed several droplets of sweat on Sir Richard's forehead, then patches of wet at his armpits.

'What else do you expect me to do?' Sir Richard shouted. 'I have absolutely no options here. Tell me. What else can I do?'

Danny heard himself say, 'You have to murder a fourteen-year-old boy, Sir Richard.'

Sir Richard's face twitched. Danny felt stupid saying what he'd said, but he thought it might spook Sir Richard to spell it out.

After another pause, Sir Richard said, 'You're a fan, aren't you? A City fan.'

'Yes,' Danny managed. He looked at the floor. He

wasn't listening properly. He was trying to work out if he could overpower Sir Richard. If he was quick, he could get to the gun first. But he still couldn't move. His body was paralysed.

'If you'd just stayed out of it, Roberts would have been on the plane to the finals in a fortnight,' Sir Richard went on. 'A more valuable player than ever after all the kidnapping publicity. I . . . the club would have made millions out of merchandise and promotional opportunities . . . I am doing this for the club.'

Danny felt numb. Sir Richard sounded like a child explaining why he'd done something wrong.

'If you had just kept out of it, it would have been fine. The club would have been better off. Champions League next season. A couple of new players. If only you knew who we're trying to sign. You wouldn't believe it. Half the players in Spain and Italy want to play alongside Roberts.'

Danny said nothing. He just stared at Sir Richard, his brow low over his eyes, trying to hide the fact that he was paralysed with fear.

'I thought you should know why. I don't believe anyone knows where you are. Otherwise they'd be here.' Sir Richard cleared his throat. 'Andy? ANDY?'

The door opened.

'Boss?'

'Take him to the basement. The generator room. I need to think what to do with him.'

'Roberts has seen him, boss.'

'I know.'

'So . . .'

'So what?'

Andy went over to Sir Richard and whispered something in his ear.

Sir Richard looked at Danny, furious. 'If I let you go, you'll ruin everything. If I kill you, Roberts will ask questions. What am I going to do with you?'

Sir Richard actually sounded as if he was really was asking Danny's opinion.

'Take him down to the generator room, Andy. I have to think.'

Andy stared back at Sir Richard.

'Yes, he's a kid, Andy! I am fully aware of that fact. Do you think I want to do this? But we need to. Do you want twelve years for kidnap and attempted murder? Because, Andy, it's us or him.'

Danny felt his shoulder being grabbed. He was spun round. He was surprised Andy had been able to move him he felt so rooted to the spot. Then he saw Andy pick up the gun and felt a firm push on his back.

A PLACE OF EXECUTION

'Lift,' Andy said, pushing Danny ahead of him. 'Press the button.'

Danny pressed the button. It occurred to him that he was not as afraid as he should be. Instead he felt numb. Like he wasn't there at all. That his arms and legs did not belong to him. That someone else was making him do the things he did.

The lift door opened. Danny stepped in. Andy paused just outside the lift door, the gun in his hand. Danny willed the door to close. Then he could be on his own.

But Andy stepped into the lift.

'Look, kid. I don't want to do this. But ... Oh, forget it. Just press the button.'

Danny still felt far away. Utterly pliant. But something was breaking through.

A voice in his head telling him to do something.

But not his voice. And it was quiet at first.

A part of Danny felt it would be easier to go along

with what was going to happen. Down to the basement. Along the corridor with the man with the gun. Do what he was told. That felt the easiest, almost the most comfortable thing to do. Then he thought of his mum, his dad, his sister.

And then he realized whose voice was breaking through.

His sister's.

What would she say to him now?

'Danny. Get your finger out. Do something. Don't be such a wimp all your life.'

The voice was louder now.

Something flickered in Danny. If Emily was here, she'd kick ass. That's what she'd do. He'd spent his whole life trying not to be like her. Maybe for once he *should* try to be like her.

'What are you waiting for?' Andy said. 'I told you to press the button.'

Danny pressed the second-floor button.

'Not that one.'

Danny pressed the second-floor button again.

Andy pushed Danny aside – slamming him against the side of the lift, hollow metal thundering – and pressed the basement button.

'Bottom floor,' Andy said, still pressing the basement button. His other hand was on Danny, pinning him to the side of the lift.

Danny felt the motion of the lift going down. Smooth. Barely noticeable.

The doors began to open. Second floor.

Andy pushed the doors-close button. But the doors continued to open. He punched the button again. Violent now. Under pressure. A different man to the one who'd been arguing with Sir Richard.

This was Danny's only chance.

It happened before he could think it through. He shoved Andy hard with his shoulder, putting the weight of his whole body into it and the power of his rage at Sir Richard. A man he'd trusted – worshipped, even – a fraud.

Andy went flying, sprawling outside the lift, his gun skittering across the floor, bouncing off the wall. Danny saw the carpet beneath him. City badges. Club colours. Andy looked back at him, paralysed for a second.

Danny pressed the doors-close button.

The doors closed. The lift started to move. Danny was alone. He had seconds – two or three – to think. His mind was alert now. What next? He could get off at the first floor or in the basement. He had no idea where the stairs were. Except that the basement stairs were next to the lift doors.

Then it came to him. Crystal clear. In the book *The Maltese Falcon*, Sam Spade loses a tail by sending the lift to the basement, but getting off the floor before.

The lift had just passed the first floor. Danny punched the ground-floor button. He felt the lift stop. The doors opened. It was a miracle. He'd hide on the ground floor.

Before he ran, he punched the basement button and the doors-close button then sprinted out on to the floor where he'd been to the press conference and straight through the doors into the room. He let the door close softly, then waited. Listening.

Now what?

Danny stood with his back against the wall, looking at the darkened room. He could hear himself breathing. And – although he was in the greatest danger he'd ever been in in his life – he felt euphoric. But Danny knew this was just adrenalin. So he breathed deeply. In and out. In and out. Preparing for what would come next.

A few seconds later, Andy arrived at the lift, hammering on the doors. Through a crack in the door, Danny saw him watching the number change to basement on the small screen, then rush off, back to the staircase.

It had worked. Danny had won himself time. But now – with options – he felt more tense than ever.

He leaned with his back to the door, trying to

control his breathing, trying to work out the best thing to do. He had seconds.

How to get out?

The only way he knew was the fire exit in the basement.

He tried to remember if he'd seen a fire-escape staircase from the ground floor. There was bound to be at least one.

He pulled the door open. Softly. No one there.

He imagined that Andy would be in the basement now. Checking rooms, if Danny was lucky. On his way back, if Danny was unlucky.

Danny started to run hard.

Along the club carpet.

Past the trophy cabinets.

Past photos of the great players. One of Sam Roberts.

Where was Roberts now? Had they moved him from the cellar room too? he wondered.

Then he put Roberts out of his mind. If Sir Richard said he was safe, Danny believed him. He had nothing to gain from harming Roberts. And, anyway, Danny had to be single-minded now. One focus. Escape.

He reached the end of the floor.

No fire exit.

A dead end.

He froze and looked behind him, expecting to see Andy.

But he was still alone.

He looked around him. He felt his panic rising, but knew he mustn't give into it.

Think.

Be clear.

Take control.

He looked for an exit, but was really disorientated.

This was no good. He felt like he was losing it.

He needed a way out. He looked again.

And there it was: a fire-exit sign, hidden down a small staircase.

He took the steps four at a time, reaching the bottom in two strides.

Two blue doors. A metal bar across them.

A sign said THIS DOOR IS ALARMED.

Danny smiled. Not half as alarmed as he was.

Would it go off?

Danny had no choice. He wasn't going to try and hide. He wanted to be outside. Free. And safe.

He pushed the doors, then ran, not even sure if he heard an alarm. He thundered down a metal staircase, across the tarmac in the dark towards the main gates into the car park. He was surprised to see the gates were open. He thought they'd still be shut, like they were two or three hours ago. But obviously they'd been opened so Sir Richard's car could get in. Of course.

And there was his car now. The red Mercedes. Danny had seen it many times outside Sir Richard's house by the park on his way to school.

Then he noticed that the headlights were on.

And it was moving. Coming towards him. Slowly at first, then faster, then very fast, with the roar of a F1 car. And Sir Richard was at the wheel.

Danny stopped. He had nowhere to go. The car was seconds away from him. He could see Sir Richard's face clearly. Not smiling with satisfaction, not laughing like a madman – just like a commuter, expressionless, on his way to work.

Danny was paralysed.

Fifteen metres. Ten metres. Five metres. And everything went quiet. Danny closed his eyes and jumped. Like a keeper facing a penalty. He felt his body thrown into the air. He was aware of pain down his side. But it didn't hurt like he thought it would.

Danny opened his eyes slowly after he heard the crash. The car had gone through one of the metal gates, one of the exits from the stadium. Then it had hit a wall. A gush of steam was spraying upwards from the punctured bonnet.

Danny was lying next to it, his feet an inch from the black tyre tracks scored on to the tarmac. He didn't know what had happened. How he'd survived. If Sir Richard was dead or alive. All he did know was that *he* was not dead, that he could walk out of the stadium and on to the main road.

And that's exactly what he did.

SUNDAY

HOME

'I wasn't happy last night, Danny.'

Mum was cross.

'I'm sorry. It was a last-minute thing,' Danny said.

'What sort of thing?'

'Paul asked me to stay over. So I did.'

'Just you and him.'

Danny knew what his mum was thinking.

Girls.

One of her friends had a son who was wild. Tom, who was forever not coming home, forever lying. Danny wanted to say he wasn't like Tom, but realized that last night he had been. And if his parents believed that he had been doing what Tom did, rather than what had really happened, it would be better. For everyone.

'So was it just you and Paul?'

'It was a party,' Danny said.

'Girls?' Mum said.

Danny's sister sniggered. She'd been standing at the

door the whole time. Enjoying the show, Danny thought. She was the one normally getting done.

'Charlotte?' Emily said.

Danny saw a faint smile on his dad's face.

'Yes. Girls,' Danny said.

'I feel let down by you, Danny. You lied.'

Danny felt hot with shame as Mum walked out of the room. This was terrible. They were cross with him because he'd lied. But they didn't know there was another, far worse lie undiscovered. He felt bad. That he'd got into this. That he'd disappointed his mum and dad. That he'd lied.

Dad left the room, adding nothing.

'I gave her your mobile number,' Emily said, still standing in the doorway.

Danny couldn't imagine what his sister was talking about. He looked at her, expecting some sort of attack or snide remark.

'You gave who my number?' he said cautiously.

'Charlotte. She asked me for it.'

'Why?' Danny said.

'Why what?'

'Why does she want it?'

'She likes you, dumb ass.'

'And why did you give her it?'

'Because I like you too. Sometimes.'

Danny was confused. Everything was on its head.

'You could have told them I smoke,' Emily said. 'But you didn't.'

Danny closed his eyes. He felt faint with tiredness. When he opened them, his sister had gone and his father was sitting next to him. He pushed a cup of tea towards Danny.

'Brew?'

'Thanks.'

Danny and his dad sat in silence. It felt good. To be next to Dad like this. Danny wished he could tell him everything. But he couldn't. Not yet.

Danny was asleep on the sofa, his father gone, when his mobile rang. He grabbed it automatically, said hello, then regretted he hadn't cleared his throat first, hoping to hear Charlotte's voice.

'Hello, Danny.'

It was a man's voice.

'Hello?' Danny said.

'Don't you know who I am?'

'No. Sorry. Who is it?'

'Have you been a good boy?'

Danny said nothing. He felt cold and vulnerable. Someone had found out his number. Andy? He was in it deep now.

'Have you been to the police, Danny boy?' the voice said.

'No.' Danny said it without thinking. It definitely wasn't Sir Richard. So it had to be Andy.

'Good.'

Danny wondered whether he should change his story, maybe suggest he had been to the police.

'Make sure you don't. And I'll see you very soon. OK?'

'OK,' was all Danny could think to say as the call was cut off.

He put the phone down.

What had he got himself into? And how did they know his number?

He had hoped it was Charlotte on the phone. If it had been, he might be getting ready for his first date with her right now. Danny almost laughed. Instead of worrying about Charlotte, he was worrying that a smoking gunman called Andy was going to come round to his house and finish him off.

His life was a mess. He was getting himself deeper and deeper into trouble. Every move he made seemed to make things worse. So should he do something about it? Or should he let it play itself out?

It was easy in the end. If he sat here and did nothing, he would only get more and more worried and he wouldn't have any better idea of what was going on.

So long as he stuck to his word — made sure he was home by 10 p.m., as he'd promised his dad — he had to do something.

Danny went to the computer. There was someone he could contact.

GOODFELLAS

Outside the football stadium it was the same as it had been all week. Ranks of television vans. Journalists waiting outside the gates to the main stand. Queues of fans at the club shop buying their Sam Roberts shirts. And the shrine to the missing footballer, stacked with flowers and footballs.

Danny stood at a distance and watched it all, two streams of traffic roaring between him and the stadium. He had thought about trying to change his appearance again. But he had no hair left to cut.

So now he was standing two hundred metres away from the bus stop where he said he'd meet the journalist he'd spoken to only two days ago at the first press conference. Anton Holt.

Danny had got his number off the Internet and phoned him. He said that, yes, he did have something more he wanted to tell Holt. And they'd arranged to meet at the bus stop outside the stadium ten minutes before the club's daily 11 a.m. press conference.

Danny knew he would be safe if he got to Holt first. He could tell him the story, then go to the press conference with him. And he knew he had to move fast too. It had to be this morning. Before Sir Richard had a chance to make another move. Or before whoever had phoned him that morning found him.

Danny recognized Holt at the bus stop. Young. Slim. Dark hair swept back. And in a suit.

Danny walked over the road, a break in the traffic appearing just when he needed it.

Holt asked no questions as Danny told him his story. He just nodded. And looked concerned. Danny had expected him to take notes. But he didn't.

When Danny had finished talking, Holt said nothing.

'You don't believe me, do you?' Danny said, suddenly feeling vulnerable.

What had made him trust this man? Maybe he was on Sir Richard's books too. Maybe all the media were. And it was just a big conspiracy to sell newspapers as well as football shirts.

'It's my job to listen,' Holt said. 'Then to find out if what people say is true. I want to believe you. But I need more.'

'That's why I wanted to come to the press conference with you. We can confront Sir Richard. He's destroying the club.'

'But you can't just go and throw accusations around like that.'

'What? Why?' Danny's plan was in pieces.

'I can't go into a press conference in front of the world's TV cameras without a shred of proof and say, "Gawthorpe has kidnapped his own player. He's an evil villain. Oh and, by the way, Sam Roberts is in the basement. Follow me."' Anton Holt ran his hand through his hair. 'Also, there's my job. My boss is best mates with Gawthorpe. If this doesn't work out, they'll never let me in the stadium again – so how can I report on the team then?'

Danny shrugged.

'Can you give me any proof?' Holt said. 'If not, I have to look into it. It could take me a couple of days.'

Danny frowned. He wanted it solved now.

'Danny, I'm not letting you down. I want to believe you. But I need more time.'

Danny racked his brain. It occurred to him that maybe he *had* made it all up. The kidnap. The shooting. Sir Richard. The burglars. And Charlotte. Maybe he'd imagined it all. It seemed so absurd. You sometimes heard about people who had imagined a whole life and had come back to earth with a bump.

What proof was there? Danny had no photos. No recordings. There was nothing on the ground floor of the stand, where the press conference would be. Everything had happened in the basement and in Sir Richard's office. And he wouldn't get access to them.

Then it came to him. Sir Richard's car. And the gate he'd crashed into.

'His car,' Danny said.

'What?'

'Sir Richard's car. He drove it at me, but it crashed into the gate. Last night. Remember, I told you? I can show you.'

'That would do it,' Holt said. 'Come on.'

But Danny stopped Holt.

'Can we walk slowly?' Danny said. 'Just walk past the scene. I'll lead you. And don't react if you see anything. Just keep walking, so we don't stand out. Then straight into the press conference.'

Holt nodded.

Danny smiled, but his heart was thumping. It all depended on this. Everything. They had to think every move through.

They walked to the club gates. Danny just ahead of Holt.

There was no sign of Sir Richard's car. But they kept

walking. There was no glass or smashed plastic you'd see after a car accident. Danny began to feel shaky. They were twenty metres away from the gated entrance to the main stand. The gate Sir Richard had driven into. This was Danny's last chance.

He caught Holt's eye. Holt was nodding. Danny didn't know what it meant until Holt gestured with his eyes to the wall next to the gate. There were marks. Streaks. Several bricks had been shaved away, exposing lighter coloured brick. And there were streaks of red too. Sir Richard's Mercedes was red.

Danny watched Holt pull his mobile phone out to snap a photo of the damage.

They reached the door to the main entrance. A huddle of journalists were going through.

'Say nothing,' Holt said.

Danny nodded.

All the journalists were signing in. Danny panicked. Did he have to sign in? If he did, his hands would shake so much, he'd drop the pen. He never signed in for anything before. And now there was a queue of journalists behind him.

Holt looked back at him again. He must have sensed Danny's fears.

'It's OK. I've got it sorted. Trust me.'

Danny waited, completely in Holt's hands.

Holt went to sign in.

'Who's the boy?' a woman in a suit asked Holt.

'Work-experience kid. School placement. That OK? They wanted him to see something real.'

She let them pass.

They climbed up a staircase and entered the inside of the stand in the middle. Danny looked down to his right to the small staircase he'd run down before, then left to the lifts he'd escaped from six hours ago. He felt a chill of fear. The sickness he'd felt last night when he'd thought he wasn't going to get out. He looked around for Sir Richard or Andy. There was no sign of them. He looked for security cameras and saw two.

Holt stopped outside the press-conference room door.

'One call,' Holt said, holding his hand up.

Danny waited in silence, watching the journalists file into the press-conference room. Some in jeans and T-shirts, some in suits. Men and women. Old and young. And at the end of the room, the table with several microphones and a backcloth advertising the club sponsor, Sir Richard's scrap company.

'Rebecca? It's Anton. Listen. Can you get someone to check car-repair garages for a red Merc? Front and side crash damage. There's not many red Mercs in the city.' Holt paused to listen. 'Sir Richard? I couldn't possibly comment.' Holt smiled broadly as he closed his phone.

'Right, Danny. We listen to what they have to say. See if any of the other journos have anything interesting to ask. Then I stand up. I tell your story. Get that copper over there to join us. And you lead us to the bunker. Yeah?'

Danny felt an explosion of nerves. Him leading dozens of people to the bunker. It sounded unreal. But this was his moment. He tried to imagine he was a real detective about to reveal all. But that didn't help. It just made him feel even more nervous.

'Yeah,' Danny said, his voice wobbling.

'Let's go in, then.'

Danny followed Holt into the press conference. He didn't see Sir Richard watching him from a doorway to the left. Nor the look of surprise on Sir Richard's face.

THE CHALLENGE

The press-conference room was full again. There were at least fifty journalists. Three cameras at the back, lights reflecting off their lenses. Two on tripods. One on a woman's shoulder.

When Danny saw Sir Richard enter the press conference he almost retched. He saw him from behind. His silver hair. His black jacket. A green folder tucked under his arm.

Holt put his hand on Danny's back. 'Are you OK, Danny?'

Danny felt weak and hot. 'Not really. But I can cope. It's just seeing him.'

The sight of the man who had said he might kill him – in the very building where he'd said it – was almost too much for Danny. He remembered his years of dreaming about being a private detective. He'd never imagined feeling like this. He resolved that when this was over he'd go back to a quiet life. Trying out for the school football team. Asking Charlotte out. Those were the kinds of risks he wanted to face. After this.

Danny watched Sir Richard sit down next to the senior policewoman. Just the two of them this time. Danny had thought he'd feel fear seeing him again, but his overwhelming feeling was hatred. Towards this man and what he was doing.

He couldn't imagine what they were going to say when he spoke out. Would his investigations have any effect on them at all?

'Good morning, everybody,' the policewoman said, sitting down and waiting for Sir Richard to sit down. As the noise of the journalists subsided, she played with her hair at the back. Smoothing it. 'Thank you for coming. Especially on a Sunday. I am pleased to say that we have some encouraging news.'

Encouraging news? Danny wondered what was going on. What could have changed? Part of him was fascinated to see how Sir Richard was going to get out of the situation he was in. What could he possibly say or do?

Danny looked around the room. There was a silence. An expectation. Then, looking back at the table where the policewoman was pausing, Danny saw Sir Richard staring right at him. A cold hard stare. Danny felt Holt's arm go round him and noticed Holt stare back at Sir Richard, who looked away.

'Overnight Sir Richard received a communication from the I.K.G.P.,' the policewoman went on. 'They are offering to negotiate and Sir Richard has accepted. We hope in the next twenty-four hours to have good news. But until then I must ask those of you who are engaged in undercover work – you know who you are – to desist. This is a sensitive period. Any journalists who take their enquiries any further, thus jeopardizing our negotiations, will be met with the full force of the law.'

Fifty hands went up. A barrage of questions. But the policewoman went on, raising her voice. 'I have heard that one of the newspapers has put up a reward of one million pounds for information leading to Roberts' rescue. I want this knocked on the head right now. This investigation is at a delicate stage. Anyone trying to solve this crime on their own will only make things worse. They could be putting Roberts' life in danger. I'd like to ask the newspaper to take back its offer.'

The hands shot up again, as if they hadn't heard the policewoman's last words.

'Sir Richard? Will Roberts be back in time to train with the England squad?'

'Sir Richard? Are you going to pay the ransom?'

'Sir Richard? How much is it now?'

'I have asked Sir Richard not to answer any questions until the matter is resolved,' the policewoman said.

'Can I make a statement, rather than ask a question?'

Danny stared at Holt. He had spoken sooner than Danny had imagined he would.

This was it.

Danny felt his mouth go dry. He wanted to breathe deeply, but his breaths were short and shallow.

'Yes,' the policewoman said. 'So long as it doesn't jeopardize the recovery of Sam Roberts. If it does, then my previous statement stands.'

'Anton Holt, *Evening Post*,' Holt said. 'One of my sources has given me information to suggest that Sam Roberts is, in fact, here at City Stadium.'

Conversations muttered throughout the room. Questions. Laughter.

'That's absurd,' Sir Richard said. 'I . . .'

The policewoman put her hand over Sir Richard's microphone. 'No more,' she mouthed to him, then turned to Holt. 'Explain,' she said, over the noise that had increased.

Danny could sense Sir Richard's eyes boring into him. But he didn't look up. He just stared at his hands as his fingers intertwined with each other. Like the night before, he felt he wasn't inside his body, like he wasn't here at all.

Holt stood up. And Danny noticed a quiet in the room again. But a different quiet. Nobody was moving.

Or speaking. Everyone was looking at Holt. Waiting. As if *they* had all held their breath.

'I have information that Sam Roberts is being held in a basement apartment directly beneath the main stand, accessible via the electrics room.' Holt was talking quickly. And Danny realized that he must be nervous too. 'My sources tell me that there is one man guarding him. That man is armed. That man has fired a gun. I have seen physical evidence that backs up this story. My source described to me an incident with a car outside last . . .'

People had stopped listening to Holt. The room was on its feet.

Holt stopped talking.

'Wait. Stop,' Sir Richard said, as most of the journalists headed for the door. He was pale and sweating, his eyes bearing down on Danny.

'Please . . .' the policewoman said.

But it was too late. The room was emptying. Dozens of men and women charging out of the door, towards the staircase Danny had walked down two days before.

Danny stayed close behind Holt, catching Sir Richard's eye again. He couldn't be sure, but he thought Sir Richard was trying to mouth words to him, but he couldn't make them out.

Fifty people were piling down the steps to the

basement. To Danny it was familiar, like leaving the football after a good win. There was an electricity in the air. An excitement.

As he made his way down to the basement corridor, Danny saw a forest of TV cameras and microphones. Some of the TV cameras were pointing at Holt, as Danny went along in his wake. Other journalists were waiting at the door to the electrics room. They made a space for Holt and Danny to come through.

'Let's see your mystery bunker, then, Holt,' one pink-faced and overweight journalist said, sneering.

'Danny?'

Danny looked at Holt.

Holt gestured at the door.

Danny went to open it. It was stiff again.

'Locked?' the sneering journalist said.

Then the door gave and Danny opened it. He let Holt and half a dozen other journalists into the electrics room.

The first thing Danny noticed was the moisture. There was condensation on some of the pipes that ran up the wall. The room had been dry before. Very dry.

'Go on then, Holt,' the pink-faced journalist said.

'Is this it?' Holt said.

'Yes.'

'Can you lift it?'

'Yes,' Danny said. He felt his hands shaking as he lifted the trapdoor. Heavy in his hands.

But, as he lifted it away, Danny knew something was wrong. The smell. The air. Everything.

Holt helped Danny lift the trapdoor away, to lean it against a wall. Then turned to see six journalists peering down a hole. With more behind them.

'It's just an old cellar. Looks like it's flooded too.'

'What?'

One of the journalists had pulled a small torch from his top pocket. He was shining into the hole. Danny and Holt moved to the edge. Six faces looking up at theirs as they looked down.

Water. Brown water. It had to be three metres deep.

The entire apartment had been flooded.

'It's down there,' said Danny. 'I was there. Roberts too. And a man with a gun.'

'Is this your source?' the sneering journalist said to Holt.

'One of them,' Holt said. But his voice was quiet and flat, not like Danny had ever heard it. It reminded him of his dad's voice. Disappointment, not anger.

Then Holt glanced at Danny. His eyes were full of questions.

'They've flooded it,' Danny said. 'I swear it.'

The policewoman had made it through the scrum of journalists.

'Right. What have we got?'

'Nothing,' Holt said. 'Nothing. I'm sorry for wasting your time.'

'Wasting my time? You're from the *Evening Post*, yes?'

'Yes,' Holt said.

'I know your boss. Giles Forshaw. I'll be calling him.'

'Yes,' Holt said.

Holt gestured to Danny to go with his eyes. Danny shook his head.

'Go,' Holt mouthed.

Danny gave him a look, trying to say sorry. Holt looked gutted.

So Danny left the electrics room, ignoring the questions the other journalists threw at him. Moving through the cameras and microphones, past the journalists making calls into their mobile phones, laughing at Anton Holt's expense.

There was no sign of Sir Richard or Andy.

Danny pushed through the fire doors, walking this time, not running. He didn't care if an alarm went off.

It didn't anyway.

He had thought he'd be worried leaving the stadium, even scared. But all he could think of was Holt's face. That defeated look. And the things the policewoman and other journalists had been saying to him. Danny wondered if he'd destroyed Holt's career. He felt sick.

As he passed through the stadium gates, Danny looked up to the main stand, and the huge plate glass windows that allowed fans to look out across the city.

Standing in the window was Sir Richard, looking into the middle distance, talking animatedly into his mobile phone.

WE MEET AGAIN

Danny moved quickly, crossing the main road in front of a small white van that slowed down and waved him across. He waved back, waiting on the white line for three cars coming the other way to go past, then went across to the front of the chip shop and up a side street.

He needed space to think. But not near the football stadium. It wasn't safe. Nor at home, where he'd just get question after question.

Danny walked briskly. He'd find a back street. Somewhere he could collect his thoughts. He remembered the park at the back of the electrical store, where he'd been watching the burglars. A playground and a line of benches looking out over the city. No one would find him there. Sir Richard. Andy. Anton Holt. His dad. He would have time to think. Time to work out how to find a way out of the mess he'd got himself into.

He reached the park and sat with his back to the road. In front of him was the city, with the stadium in the foreground and a forest on a rising hill in the background. Vast green spaces. People in the distance, walking dogs, jogging, playing with children. A view he'd have relished a few days ago. But now he was so buried in his thoughts he barely registered it.

The sun was warm. The bench dry. Clouds scudding across the sky.

So what was he supposed to do now? Go to the police? Go on the run? Or just go home?

He wondered if it was wise to go to the police – after what had happened at the stadium. They were probably more keen to speak to him than he was to them. What was it called? Wasting police time? What was the punishment for that?

Even worse, Danny couldn't get the look on Anton Holt's face out of his mind.

He would write a letter to him once all this was over. To apologize. To say that he'd never meant to cause him so much trouble.

Most of all, Danny wished he could just go back to a normal life. No Sam Roberts. No Anton Holt. No Sir Richard. No nobody.

His mobile buzzed in his pocket.

What was this?

A text. An unrecognized number.

He immediately felt dread. Was this another anonymous message? Something malevolent.

danny. want to meet up? charlotte xxx

Danny smiled. Maybe there was one person he'd like to see after all. He felt happy for a half-second, lifted out of the mire he was stuck in.

It was funny. All this stuff with Charlotte was nowhere near as frightening as it had been a few days ago. What was scary about liking a girl, wanting to meet up with her, after what he'd been through?

He texted back:

yes. when? where? danny

Should he add a kiss? Even though she had added three, he didn't dare.

He pressed send and slipped his phone back into his pocket. Something nice to think about.

It was then that he felt himself being lifted from behind. Pulled from under each arm. A violent jolt that tore at his shoulder muscles. He could smell smoke and stale alcohol. Danny struggled, managing to get his legs under the bench, to stop himself being lifted. But he was pulled with such force over the back of the bench, there was nothing he could do. His legs gave way. He was on the floor, then he felt a blow to his head – almost knocking him out – and he was being held by his shoulders and his legs. Two men were gripping him tightly. There was no escape. Then he saw the back of a small white van, open. And, of all things, he noticed a City sticker on the back window. They hauled him into the back of the van.

Then one of the men followed him in. Danny lay with his eyes screwed up. He could feel hands going through his pockets. Painful jabs to his groin and legs.

Then he was alone. The doors slammed shut. And locked.

Two more slams as two shapes behind a metal grille got into the two front seats. The engine started and the van headed off, going through the gears in hard, short, jerky movements.

Danny sat up, then fell over as the van lunged round a corner.

He sat up again and felt his head. It felt wet. As if it was bleeding.

It was Andy. Plus another. Maybe the other guy he'd seen the night he spotted Roberts, the one who looked like a banker? They were driving him who knew where. Not back to the stadium, he was sure of that. They were heading uphill, away from the stadium and away from the city.

He tried the back door of the van. There was no lever to open it with. He lay on his back and pushed the doors with his legs, but it was no good.

After a few minutes the ride became more bumpy. Danny knew what this meant. They'd come off the main road and were on a track. It certainly wasn't a tarmacked street.

His heart was pounding. He felt shaky. Of all the scrapes he'd got into over the last week, this was the only one he couldn't see a way out of. Andy was taking him out to some remote spot. Maybe to shoot him.

Danny vomited. The stench filled the small space of the back of the van.

Danny looked up at the shapes of Andy and his companion. He could hear them talking. Laughing.

Then the van stopped.

This was it.

Danny knew it.

He told himself to be calm. Not to panic.

There had to be a way out of this.

The screen between the driver and Danny opened. 'Hello again.'

Two men. Danny stared. Neither was Andy.

So who were they?

Had Sir Richard called in some other henchmen to finish him off when he'd seen him leaving the stadium.

No. That wasn't it. This was nothing to do with Sir Richard.

Danny almost laughed.

The two men smiling at him from the front of the van were the burglars he'd met – or *nearly* met – on Friday. The shorter, moustached man on the left. An intelligent twinkle in his eye. The larger man. Heavy set. Hard looking. Not as confident as his friend.

'You're a TV star,' the larger man said.

'We were watching the newsflash. Cameras all over City. And there you are. Following some sad-case journalist who reckons he's found Roberts. Different haircut, of course. But you all the same.'

Danny kept quiet. He was their prisoner. Just like when Andy had had him, he had to be civil. Not annoy them.

'So, you're a City fan?'

'Yes,' Danny said. This was a chance. Maybe they'd go easy on him as he was a City fan.

'That's a shame, isn't it?'

'How do you mean?'

'Well, we might have to sort you out. And us being City fans too. It's a shame. That's all.'

'But first things first,' the smaller man said. 'Have you got the footage?'

'Yes,' Danny said.

'Where?'

'At home.' Danny was being as up front as he could. Trying to get them to take his word. He knew the film was his chance to escape. 'You can have it.'

'Damn right we can. And what else have you got?'

'Nothing. It's just the notebook and the camera. And you've got the notebook.' Danny remembered the chart and map on his wall, tracking the burglaries. He decided not to mention that.

'So what are we going to have to do to get the film, Danny? And how do we know you'll keep your mouth shut after that?'

Danny could sense a threat coming. But he didn't feel nervous. He actually felt elated. Had the van been driven by Andy, he'd be in a much worse situation than he was now. He felt sure he could get out of this one.

'Because you'll know where I live. I'll take you there.'

'Then there's Charlotte too, of course,' the smaller man said. 'Nice text here.'

'What?'

'This text: "the leisure centre? in an hour? charlotte". And three kisses, Danny. That sounds promising. If we let you go once we have the film, that is.'

'And if you don't have it,' the other man said, 'we could text Charlotte. Arrange for her to meet you. Except you wouldn't be there.'

Danny felt a rage coming over him. Were they

threatening to do something to Charlotte? But he had to keep a lid on it. Think, he told himself. Think.

And then it came to him. A way out of this. And out of everything else.

Maybe he could turn this around and make his kidnap by these two burglars the best thing that had ever happened to him.

TEAMWORK

'Can I ask you something?' Danny said.

'Sure you can,' said the larger man. 'Then we'll go to your house, get the film and, if you don't have it, we'll break your legs.'

Danny closed his eyes, trying not to be overwhelmed by his fear. He looked into the front of the van to calm himself.

'We don't have time for this, Danny. We need get to your house, Danny.'

'*I* know where Sam Roberts is,' Danny said.

For a second the two men were quiet.

'Yeah? Well, go and collect the one million reward.'

'I would. But I need your help.'

'Come on. Let's get out of here. This kid is starting to annoy me.' It was the large man who spoke this time.

'You can have the reward,' Danny said.

The big man started the engine. But the other put

his hand up. 'Hold on. Let's hear him out, Neil. He was there today, remember.'

Neil. Danny memorized the larger man's name. It was a slip by the smaller man.

The engine cut.

'Go on.'

Danny told them the story of the last few days. Beginning with his encounter with them. Both men listened. No interruptions. Danny tried to tell the story briefly. Not adding anything the men didn't need to know. As he spoke he felt himself getting more and more animated. He hated Sir Richard. He wanted these two men to help him get back at the man who'd nearly killed him.

'I dunno. If you didn't find him today, he'll be long gone. And that's if you're not lying to us.'

Danny nodded. It had been a long shot, expecting two burglars to change from wanting to do him over to joining him on what appeared to them to be a fool's errand.

'Wait a minute, Tony. I did see the people carrier he mentioned. That's why I left him in the yard and ran for it. I thought it was one of them unmarked CID cars.'

Tony. Tony and Neil. He had both their names now.

'You saw it?' Tony said.

'I did. And I wondered why it was going into the stadium at that time.'

Tony went quiet. Nobody interrupted his silence. 'Let's say it's true,' he said eventually. 'Roberts was in the stadium. I can believe it of Gawthorpe. But by now he's going to be long gone. Once Gawthorpe got wind of you, he'd have got him out of there. Right away.'

'Yeah,' said Neil.

'So if he has,' said Danny, 'then the stadium will be deserted. That gunman will be long gone too. But . . . if he is still there – and we can get in and do something about it – that's one million pounds for you. Either way you can't lose.'

'So what did you do today?' Danny's dad said.

The whole family was sitting round the table. Fish, chips and peas.

Earlier, when the burglars had given him his phone back, Danny had texted Charlotte to put her off until tomorrow. He told her to watch the evening news, saying then she'd know he had a good excuse. This time he left a single 'x' after his name.

'Nothing much,' said Emily. 'What about you, Danny? Did you have a good day? Did you see anyone nice?'

Danny was staring out of the window, watching a squirrel walk upside down underneath a branch, a thousand thoughts whirling round his brain. He felt in his pocket for the small digital camera tape he'd put there.

'No,' said Danny.

Danny's mind was on 7 p.m. That's when the burglars were coming to collect him two streets away. He'd agreed to hand over the film. Then they'd go to City Stadium together and find a way in.

'I played football,' Danny said.

'Did you win?' Danny's mum asked.

'No. We lost.' Danny thought they'd be more likely to believe him if he said they'd lost.

'But did you see *her*?' Emily smirked.

Danny's parents said nothing.

'No. But she texted me. Thanks for that, Emily.'

Emily looked shocked Danny was being so up front.

'We might meet tonight.'

'In that case,' Danny's dad offered, 'you can have an extended time tonight. Until eleven?'

'No. We said ten and I'll stick to it,' Danny said.

'Let's say ten thirty,' Mum suggested. 'Then it gives you more time.'

Emily laughed. Her mouth full. 'To do what?' she said, food spilling out on to the table.

Danny waited on the corner of Foxglove Avenue and North Lane, standing back under a tree in the shadows.

He was wearing all black clothes, as instructed by the burglars.

Five past seven.

Ten past seven.

Quarter past seven.

No sign of the burglars.

As he waited, Danny's mind started to drift.

The first thing to occur to him was what on earth was he doing? Meeting up with two burglars who had only earlier today kidnapped him and threatened him. And now he was going with them to break into a place that had at least two people in it that wanted to see him dead.

And why was he doing it?

He wasn't sure any more.

Maybe it was because he wanted to be a private detective. Maybe it was because he wanted to save Sam Roberts. Maybe it was because he wanted to prove to Anton Holt that he was telling the truth. He didn't know. He could give reason after reason. The only thing he knew was that he wanted to solve this mystery, even if he had to go back into that stadium.

At last the van arrived. Danny sat in between the two men. He saw a baseball bat lodged between Neil's knees.

They drove for about ten minutes, then stopped, both staring at Danny.

'Film,' said Tony.

Danny patted his pockets, found the film and handed it over.

'And you've got your camera?' Neil said.

Danny nodded.

'Let's see it.'

Danny handed it over.

'Show us the film,' Neil said, handing it back.

Danny slipped the tape into the camera, pocketing the blank he'd put in there for tonight. Also as instructed.

He searched and found the footage of the burglars. The three of them sat in the front seat of the van watching the small screen. Nobody spoke. The smaller man laughed at one point. Danny felt like he was watching one of those TV shows about dodgy workmen with his mum and dad, sat on the sofa.

'That's a good film, Danny,' said Tony. 'Very nice. You don't have any copies, do you?'

'No.'

'How do we know that?' said Neil. Hardness in his voice again.

'You don't,' said Danny. 'You'll have to trust me.'

Tony laughed. 'Promise us, then.'

'Promise?' Neil said. 'What's that worth?'

'I reckon it's worth a lot to Danny,' Tony said, with a hint of malice. 'Eh, Danny?'

'I promise I have made no copies. I promise that's the only one,' Danny said.

'That's good enough for me,' said Tony, starting the engine. 'Let's go.'

Neil pulled a face.

They steered out on to the main road.

'Right. Here's the deal,' Tony said. 'We're going to search the entire stadium.'

'The whole stadium?' Neil said.

'That's right. The two of us do all the work. Breaking in. Searching every room. Everything. And you, Danny, film it. That's all you do. Got it?'

'Sure,' said Danny.

'Then, if we do find anything, we've got the proof,' Tony said. 'And a nice little film to show the grandkids too.'

Ten minutes later the stadium came into view, rearing up from behind rows of terraced houses.

Danny felt anxious. This would be his third trip into the bowels of City Stadium. The last two times he could easily have been killed.

'This is it, boys,' Tony said, changing down a gear. 'We're going in.'

THE COMPANY OF STRANGERS

In a car, parked in front of Hand of Cod, a man was waiting. He was in his late twenties and dark-haired. On one knee he had a notepad and a pen. On the other a mobile phone.

Anton Holt.

He was listening to Five Live. The commentary of England's first pre-tournament warm-up game. Denmark away. England was dominating the game – like the tournament second favourites should – but they just couldn't convert their dominance into goals. There was no one to put the ball in the back of the net.

'England miss Roberts even more tonight,' said the commentator. 'The attack is short on goals, short on class.'

When Holt saw the small white van go past the entrance to the stadium for a second time, he knew something was going on. He could tell it was the same van because of the City sticker in the back window.

This was what he had been waiting for. He turned down the radio, so he could concentrate his mind.

The van took a left up a side street. Holt waited, staring at the space between his car and where the van had disappeared. He was rewarded soon enough, seeing two men and a boy cross the road and go alongside a Portakabin yard.

Holt smiled. There was something about Danny's story that still had him gripped. He knew there was more to it than a boy's overactive imagination.

But what was Danny up to now?

Danny pointed to the hole in the fence. He saw Neil nod at him, smiling. This was where they'd first met. Danny had never dreamed they'd come here again. Together. He looked at Neil's baseball bat and felt pleased they were on the same side tonight.

Tony indicated that no one was to talk by putting his finger over his lips. Then he took a small pair of wire cutters out of his pocket and began to clip away at the wire fence until there was a hole big enough for all three of them to pass through, one by one.

Then – as they'd agreed – Danny led them round the back of the Portakabins and the central yard, avoiding the sensors that would set off the security lights and give them away.

They reached the fence on the far side of the yard

and saw the stadium. There were no cars or vans in the car park. City Stadium looked empty.

Danny was reminded of his first night here. Hiding from the two men who were with him now. Tonight it was warmer and lighter. The air smelled of pollen. Danny remembered the old woman's garden nearby. He wondered if it was her flowers they could smell.

Tony cut through the next fence quickly, making a gap they could just squeeze through, but that he could disguise as if it wasn't there once they were on the other side.

Neil went first. Down the grassy slope quickly, then hitting the hard tarmac of the car park at the bottom. Danny slipped and nearly sprained his ankle. But he didn't cry out. He didn't pull a face. He just paused, checked his footing and kept going.

Everything had to be done in silence, as they'd agreed.

Now they were behind the bins where Danny had hidden yesterday.

Danny had told Neil about the door. How it worked. How he'd got in before. Tony went over to it, pushed the door gently and tried to get his fingers round the edge. But he came back quickly.

'It won't move. I'll have to go in through a window, then come down and let you in.'

Neil nodded.

'A window?' Danny said.

'Start filming now,' Tony said, putting a finger to his lips.

Danny took out his camera and flicked it on.

He filmed the smaller of the two men walking to the corner of the stadium. He was looking up at the window, his eyes scanning every part of the facade. He paced up and down, as if undecided. Then he stopped. Danny could just make out his mouth moving, as if he was talking to himself.

'He's spotted one,' Neil said. 'Watch him go now. Make sure you get it on film.'

Danny zoomed in as Tony kneeled to tighten his shoelaces, then stood to put both hands on one of the huge drainpipes that came down from the top of the main stand. And then he was off. Shimmying up the drainpipe.

Against the facade of the stand he looked tiny. He was up ten, fifteen metres in seconds. Danny had to arch his back as he tried to keep him in focus. Then Tony reached across and placed his foot on a ledge underneath a small square window. Danny tried to calculate where he'd be. In the toilets outside the main bar area, he thought.

Tony's hands searched in the small gap to find the catch and lifted the window open with ease.

And then – like a rabbit down a hole – he disappeared.

Danny couldn't believe it.

'That was amazing,' he said.

'He's a genius. You should see what he can do. And he's so small and light, he can . . .'

Suddenly there was a siren.

'Down,' said Neil.

Danny crouched behind the bins. It was a police car. Hiding, they heard its siren coming nearer, up the main road from the city centre. They waited. Expecting the worst. Wondering what Tony was doing and if he'd heard it.

Danny assumed he'd set off an alarm in the stadium. The police would be on them in seconds. He looked around for a way out.

The siren was loud now, echoing off the far end of the stadium. For a second they saw the flashing lights as the police car sped past the main gates of the stadium and carried on away from them.

'We were lucky there,' said Neil. 'I thought we were toast.'

'Me too.'

Thirty seconds later the door at the end of the stand opened. Tony beckoned them in. As agreed, Danny began filming again, making sure he got shots of them entering the stadium.

Danny pointed to the place where the bullet had hit the breezeblock on the first night.

The two men grinned.

'I don't think there's anyone here,' whispered Tony eventually. Not down here, anyway. But let's make sure.'

Cautiously, they searched each room. Dressing rooms. Referee's room. Laundry room. Tony opened the doors and edged round the corner. Neil followed up with his baseball bat hanging at his side, Danny filming it all.

Then they came to the electrical room.

'This was the one,' Danny whispered.

'We should check it,' Tony said.

'The door handle's stiff,' Danny said. 'Do it slowly.'

He filmed the smaller man easing the handle open. The crack it made as it opened was not loud, but to Danny it seemed like an explosion.

There was nothing in the room, apart from the lights of the fuse boxes flashing and the dials turning.

Danny pointed to the trapdoor, then filmed as Neil opened it.

'There's no water,' he said, shining his torch down the hole.

'What?' asked Danny.

'There's no water. Just a right mess.'

Danny followed the two men down through the

hole in the floor. The ladder was slippery with mud and moisture. Danny's hands were wet and slimy when he finally reached the bottom.

What had once been an underground apartment – holding an international footballer – was now a disaster area. The main room and three bedrooms were complete chaos. Furniture all over the place. Stains on the walls. And Danny saw two rats scuttling along the skirting boards. The air smelt damp and dirty. Earthy. The TV was tipped over, the widescreen face up, collecting drips of water from above. The bedrooms were filthy. Sheets and pillows and carpets, brown and stinking. Danny filmed it all.

Neil checked each bedroom thoroughly. There was no sign of Sam Roberts. Danny had half expected to see his drowned body on one of the beds.

'Let's go up to the next floor.'

It took ten minutes to check the ground floor. The press-conference room. The hospitality suites. A long corridor of offices.

Nothing.

They moved cautiously to the next floor. Moving up the staircase, one step at a time, listening between each footstep.

As they reached the second floor, Tony put his hand out.

'I heard something,' he whispered.

'What?'

'Voices.'

He crept up the next staircase and put his head round the first corner, darting back immediately.

'There's a light. And two men, I think. I can hear their voices.'

'No,' said Neil.

'No? What do you mean "no"? This could be our chance. Are you forgetting the one million quid?'

'No,' said Neil. 'We just need to be careful. Whoever's up there is armed, right?'

'Right,' said Danny.

'Here's what we do,' Tony said. 'I go up first. Then Neil. Then Danny. I do the looking. Neil has the baseball bat ready. Danny films it all. OK?'

'OK.'

They came to the first corner of the stairs, up to the third and final floor. Nobody was there, but the light was brighter and the voices were clear now.

'Someone's on the phone,' Tony whispered.

'Gawthorpe?'

'Right.'

They moved up to the next corner of the stairwell. The smaller man waved them back.

'This is it,' he said. 'I can hear two voices. Definitely.'

'Roberts?'

'No. I don't think so.'

Then there was a click.

Everything went quiet.

No voices.

'A gun,' Tony said.

'That's right,' said a voice from beneath them.

'Spot on,' said a voice above them.

Danny held the camera ahead of him. Pointing up, pointing down. But his hands were shaking. He looked imploringly to Tony, then Neil. What next?

'Come on up.' The voice was Sir Richard's. 'I've got armed men below and above you. You've no way out. And I assume – I hope – you've got young Danny with you. If you have, we can do a deal.'

CRIME AND PUNISHMENT

Danny felt sick. This time there was no escape. Especially for him. Sir Richard had asked for him. By name. He looked at Neil and Tony. Both avoided looking Danny in the eye, looking at each other instead.

'Shall we?' Tony said.

'We have to,' Neil said.

'What?' Danny said, anxiety in his voice.

'I want a decision on the count of ten,' Sir Richard said. 'One . . .'

Tony looked at Danny. He had sadness in his eyes. Danny started to panic. Why would these two men – strangers, criminals – do anything but save themselves at his expense? They weren't here for him: they were here for the reward money. One million pounds.

'Two . . . three . . .'

Then Tony crouched and began to pull up his trouser

leg. Danny didn't have a clue what was happening or what was going to happen next. He felt powerless to do anything.

'Four ... five ...' Sir Richard's voice was getting louder, filled with menace.

Tony revealed his leg. And there, strapped underneath the small man's sock, was a gun.

At first Danny backed away, thinking it was for him; that the two men he'd put his trust in had been in it with Sir Richard all along. How many times had he read that in a book?

'Six ... seven ...'

'Danny. Go out with your hands up,' Tony whispered.

Danny shook his head. So this *was* a betrayal. They were going to sacrifice him.

'When you see the man with the gun up there, raise your hands even higher. OK?'

'Why?'

'Don't talk. Just do it. Trust me.'

Danny said nothing. What choice did he have? Trust them and probably die. Don't trust them and definitely die.

'Eight ... nine ...'

Danny nodded. He'd do it.

He wanted to say, What if he shoots me first? But he couldn't find the words. Tony had offered him a slight hope. A plan. That was all there was to hold on to. Some sense of structure that could get him out of a rising tide of utter panic.

'Ten . . .'

Danny walked up to the next set of stairs, his hands half up. And there was Andy, hands pointed out in front of him, a gun silhouetted against the bright lights behind him. He was grinning.

'We meet again,' he said.

Danny raised his hands slowly towards the ceiling and stepped aside, as if leaning against the wall.

Andy started to laugh.

The explosion still came as a shock to Danny. His body cramped, knees moving towards his stomach. His ears were in agony. He fell backwards and felt himself being dragged – by Neil it turned out – back into the safe space where neither Andy nor the gunman below them could get at him.

Danny looked up. Tony was breathing heavily. But smiling. His hands were shaking violently.

'I've never used that before,' he said.

And then they heard the noise. It was half screaming, half shouting. Like an animal, Danny thought.

It was Andy.

'I hit him,' Tony said. 'I shot . . . shot him.'

Then the wall above them exploded. A large hole

appeared and covered them in plaster and fragments of brick.

Outside the stadium Anton Holt was standing at the main gate. When he heard the two gunshots he tapped 999 into his phone.

'Police,' he said, then paused before giving his name and location. 'There's been a shooting in City Stadium. I'm a journalist. There are at least four people involved. Two guns, I think. I've heard two shots.'

He listened to the voice coming from his phone.

'At the main gates. I'm in a dark blue VW. T 626 EZR,' he said.

He listened again.

'No. The shooting is inside. Up in the main stand. It's clear on the ground.'

'What now?' Neil said.

The three of them had their backs to the nearside wall, so they were out of range of any more shots.

They could hear Sir Richard talking to Andy, who was crying now.

Then a voice from below.

'If you want to get out of there alive – all of you – then give up the gun. Throw it down.'

Tony signalled that nobody should speak. 'It's three

against one,' he called to Gawthorpe. 'Your mate upstairs is injured. We come down and we've got two guns and a baseball bat. You might hit one of us, but the other two will have you.'

There was no reply. Except a second bang above them. And a bigger hole. A huge triangle of plaster falling on the carpet. Bare bricks exposed.

'And I'm waiting for you up here.' Sir Richard's voice. 'And I don't believe for a minute you've two guns. Maybe you've even run out of bullets?'

Tony grinned sheepishly. 'Plenty of bullets, Sir Richard,' he said. 'One with your name on it too.'

There was a long pause. Nobody said anything. On either of the floors.

'Hand over the boy and I'll let you go,' Sir Richard said eventually. In a low voice, as if he didn't believe they'd do it. 'And how about an incentive? You think you're going to get the one million reward? You *might*. But I can *promise* you a million. Right here and now. In cash. From my personal safe. Cash. Now.'

Tony looked at Neil. Neil looked at Tony.

Danny watched them both, a sick feeling in his stomach.

'Let's have it now. In cash, right?' Neil shouted.

Danny looked at Tony, who winked at Neil and turned to put his hand on Danny's shoulder.

It was then they heard the sirens. And not just a

single police car wailing in the night. It sounded like dozens of police cars, ambulances and fire engines. All at once.

They heard a scrambling below, thought the second gunman was coming up. But nothing happened.

Tony went down the stairs, gun in front of him. Slowly.

Ten seconds later he shouted up. 'He's gone. Come down. Immediately. Get out of there.'

Danny and Neil almost fell down the stairs, joining Tony on the second floor.

The first thing Danny saw was the lights of dozens of emergency vehicles and vans through the plate-glass windows of the main stand. So many lights flashing the road and car park could have been floodlit.

'I'll cover the staircase with this gun,' Tony said. 'Neil. You cover the lift door with your baseball bat. Danny, you just lie low and film . . . if your hands aren't shaking too much.'

'So, we wait for the police to arrive?' Danny said.

'Yes. And we cover the exits in case Sir Richard is planning an escape.'

Thirty minutes later.

On the top floor, the police found Andy in the reception area outside Sir Richard's office. He'd tied his shirt round his thigh, to reduce the blood loss.

Two guns were found hidden under a cushion behind him. He was conscious.

The other gunman had been stopped by a team of six trained sharpshooters in the car park below. He'd given himself up quickly.

There was no sign of Sir Richard.

The police had searched the stadium. All they found was an open fire exit at the foot of the main stand. So the police were now searching neighbouring industrial estates.

As Danny and the two burglars talked with the police and Anton Holt – Sam Roberts emerged from a kitchen next to Sir Richard's office, where he'd been found blindfolded. He was wrapped in a blanket, a policewoman at each arm supporting him. His hair was flat, his clothes crumpled.

Danny stood up to speak to him. Roberts was, after all, the point of all this. But a paramedic put his arm across Danny's path.

'I'm sorry, son. They'll want to make sure he's OK. You have to leave him to us for now.'

Danny understood. He just stared at his hero.

And then Roberts stared back and smiled. 'You're the boy I saw the other night, aren't you?'

Danny nodded, not sure what to say.

Then Roberts was led away to an ambulance. And into the night.

MONDAY

REWARD

After school had ended, Danny was back in the Starbucks where he'd been with his father after having his hair cut. Once he'd queued for more drinks – a cappuccino and a latte – he turned to make his way through the cluster of tables and drinkers. Then Danny sat down in the empty seat next to Charlotte.

'So then what happened?' she asked.

'Then the police arrived,' Danny said. 'We had to stand in the centre of the concourse with our hands up. But then Anton Holt – the journalist I told you about – came and said I was the one trying to rescue Sam Roberts. So they took their guns off us.'

'What about Neil and the other guy ... Tony?'

'Same thing. I vouched for them,' Danny paused. 'But the police seemed to know them anyway.' He remembered seeing the police lead Tony and Neil aside, talking to them quietly. While Tony was talking to the police he'd turned to look at Danny and winked.

'Will they get the reward?'

'I don't know. I reckon the police knew them. They must have arrested them for burglary before. I'd be surprised if they did get it.'

'Is that why it wasn't on the news?' she said. 'All it said was Tony and Neil, local painter-decorators, rescue Sam Roberts. Tony and Neil. Nothing about you.'

'I wanted to stay out of it,' Danny said.

'Why?'

'My mum and dad. I had to tell them. And they weren't happy with my face being all over the newspapers and TV.'

Danny looked across at Charlotte. Her dark hair, a strand over her left eye. And the pink flush in her cheeks again. He couldn't believe he was sitting opposite her. And that she wanted to sit opposite him.

'I suppose it's a good enough excuse,' she said. 'Or a good story.'

'One of the two,' Danny said, smiling again.

'So what now?' Charlotte said.

'I wondered . . .' Danny felt doubt overcome him again.

'You wondered what?'

'If you'd like to go to see a film sometime.'

Charlotte paused. 'I might do.'

Danny's heart was pounding. He could feel a heavy pulse in his throat.

'Tomorrow?' he said.

'Go on, then.' Charlotte grinned.

When Danny got home, Dad was waiting at the door.

'Where've you been?'

'Town. For a coffee. Charlotte.'

'I've been trying to call you.'

Danny checked his phone. He'd turned it off at the café.

'Sorry. I was . . .' He had let his dad down again.

'You've got a visitor,' Dad said.

'Yeah?' Danny imagined going into the front room to see Tony and Neil eating biscuits with his mum.

'It's Sam Roberts,' Danny's dad whispered excitedly.

Danny suddenly felt nervous. Sam Roberts was waiting to talk to him. And he felt terrified.

This was the man he'd gone to all that trouble for, so why should he be scared? He'd been dodging burglars and gunmen all week. He'd just had coffee with the girl he liked more than any girl he'd liked before. Why would he be nervous of a footballer?

Because he wasn't just any footballer. Because he was Sam Roberts.

Danny paused to breathe deeply, then walked into the room.

Roberts looked smart. He was wearing a light suit and a tie. His hair was combed back. He looked like he had the night he'd won both PFA Player of the Year and Young Player of the Year twelve months ago. And he did look young. Younger than he did on TV. Younger than he had in Sir Richard's bunker.

Anton Holt was sitting on the sofa next to Roberts. And Emily was sitting at the far end of the room, her legs coiled under her on an armchair. Beaming.

Both men rose to stand.

'Danny,' said Anton Holt. 'Sam wanted to come and see you.'

Danny smiled.

All week he had been trying not to act like a kid. But now he felt like one. A stuttering football fan. In awe. Dumbstruck.

'Hello. It's nice to meet you,' Danny said.

'Again,' said Roberts.

'Again. Yes.'

Roberts stayed standing. 'Your dad has been looking after us. He told me you and him go to all the home matches.'

'We do. And a few away. When we can.'

'And he was telling me you do commentaries for him.'

'I do. But he knows what's going on really. He just needs the names. And the odd action replay.'

Danny's dad laughed. 'You reckon?'

'Have you ever been to see England play?' Roberts said.

'No,' Danny said. 'We tried phoning to get tickets when they played in the group stages. But we couldn't even get through.'

'Would you *like* to come and see England?'

Danny paused and looked at his dad, who was nodding.

'Sure,' Danny said. 'But wasn't the last friendly yesterday?'

'Nil—nil. I know. I saw the highlights, once they'd stopped asking me loads of questions. But I was thinking about the finals.'

'I'd love to, but . . .'

'I've asked your dad, Danny. He can come too. What I'd like . . .' Sam Roberts stopped speaking for a moment. He looked tired suddenly. His voice was quavering. 'What I'd like to do, Danny, is thank you. I know those two other guys got all the glory. And I know your dad has told me why he thinks you shouldn't be involved in any of that. But also I know it was you. That I owe everything to you. So I'd like to offer you tickets for all England's games. For you and your dad. And I've sorted a room in the team hotel too. For the whole tournament. If you want it. It's the very least I can do. And it would be a real pleasure to have you there, Danny.'

'Including the final?' Danny said, his jaw dropping.

'Definitely. You can see us win it.'

Two miles away – in a long-forgotten World War II bomb shelter underneath his house – Sir Richard Gawthorpe was waiting.

He'd heard the police searching his house, taking away computers and paperwork. It had infuriated him that they could just rifle through his belongings: but he knew it didn't matter. He had his main computer down here anyway. With access to all his secret offshore accounts.

He'd miss his house. And his car. But he had enough money to buy a dozen houses and a dozen cars.

The most important thing of all was that he had enough money to sit tight and wait for the moment that he could take his revenge on a boy called Danny. He didn't know his second name yet. Or his address. But it wouldn't take long.

A footballer attacked.
A criminal on the loose.
Can Danny Harte keep his eye on the ball?

FOOTBALL DETECTIVE

DEADBALL

Follow Danny to Russia as he tackles another case, in the thrilling follow-up to

FOULPLAY

puffin.co.uk